The Frenchman

ALSO BY VELDA JOHNSTON

The Frenchman

A NOVEL OF SUSPENSE

Velda Johnston

DODD, MEAD & COMPANY
New York

Library of Congress Cataloging in Publication Data

Johnston, Velda.
  The Frenchman.

  I. Title.
PZ4.J7238Fr [PS3560.0394] 813'.5'4   76-3462
ISBN 0-396-07301-8

76000793

For JAMES RANSCOMBE,
real-life international courier

Chapter 1

Joan Creighton came into her apartment house lobby that raw March afternoon, weighted with the bone-weariness to which she had become accustomed over the past few months, and opened her mailbox. There was Cousin Muffy's letter in its Alice blue envelope, with the return address embossed in ivory.

It brought her no sense of impending evil. Instead, as she carried the letter up in the elevator, she reflected with faint amusement that Muffy's stationery was like Muffy herself—naive, bland, and incongruously girlish.

Inside her apartment, oppressed by the gray light coming through the north window, she switched on the lamp beside the sofa. Three years before, soon after she had been promoted to assistant editor of *Today's Woman*, she had bought the apartment's furniture and taken over its lease from a self-styled "bachelor girl" of about forty. In those days the apartment's furniture, including a studio couch and a hassock covered in navy blue corduroy, had seemed to echo that outmoded phrase. There had even been that ultimate cliché, a reproduction of Van Gogh's sunflower hanging above the couch. Almost immediately Joan had substituted a row of Japanese prints for the Van Gogh picture. A year later, after she inherited some of her grandmother's furniture, she had replaced the studio couch with a Victorian sofa, and the hassock with two Victorian side chairs.

She sat down and opened her letter.

Muffy, it seemed, was about to take a European tour. She would land in Paris, where she would be met by a Frenchman named Paul Lescaut. "He's what they call an international courier. He doesn't just drive, but takes charge of everything. Some friends of mine here in Cleveland hired him last year, and they say he's marvelous. He'll drive me to Florence and Venice and wherever else I want to go.

"Sara was going to go with me, but she's decided at the last minute that she'll be too busy getting ready for Young Sara's wedding. Just think, this time next year I may be a great-grandmother! Now I know a trip with an old lady might not sound exciting to a young girl like you." (Young girl, Joan thought, and cast a wry glance at a gilt-framed mirror on the opposite wall. Well, perhaps to Muffy twenty-seven still seemed very young.) "But I'd be awfully happy if you'd come with me, and I'll pay for everything, of course.

"As you probably realize, there'll be a Secret Service man with us. It seems to me our State Department is awfully silly about this whole business of bodyguards. Why, Buzz has been dead for almost six years, and it's been five since I've set foot in Washington. But even though I'm going strictly incognito, this Mr. Manchester has to go along too. I haven't met him yet, but Buzz used to play golf with his father.

"We'd leave on the twenty-third, and be gone for about a month. I know this is awfully short notice, Joaney, but I hope you can come. Let me know as soon as you decide."

Again Joan looked at her reflected face, framed in its cap of short, dark red hair. Always she had been slender,

2

but now she was so thin that her gray-green eyes looked enormous in her high-cheekboned face. Since the previous November, she'd had little appetite. It was as if her affair with Brad had quite literally left a bitter taste in her mouth, making food unpalatable.

She had sought refuge in work and, sometimes, in too much vodka. Neither had proved to be more than a temporary palliative. Perhaps somewhere in Italy—on a bridge crossing a Venetian canal, or in the shadowy nave of a Florentine church—she might find that she had regained her former confident self. Chances were against it, of course. But it might be worth trying.

She crossed her apartment to the early Victorian desk, also a legacy from her grandmother, picked up the phone and dialed Eileen's number. Eileen Haskel, a formidably intelligent divorcee of fifty-odd, was managing editor of *Today's Woman.*

"I'm sorry to bother you at your apartment like this, Eileen. But I was wondering—well, if I could take a month's leave of absence."

"What for?"

"A letter from my Cousin Muffy came today. She wants me to go to Europe with her." When Eileen did not answer, Joan added, "There might be an article in it."

"Could be."

Joan understood her boss's dubious tone. Muffy could not be considered even remotely as hot news. Nearly a dozen years had passed since the end of her husband's stormy tenancy of the White House. And even in those days the consensus of Washington correspondents had been that Martha Matilda—nicknamed Muffy in early childhood—was the dullest First Lady within living memory.

"But even if there isn't an article in it," Eileen said, "I think you should go. I'm tired of seeing you drag yourself around like a sick cat, all because of that s.o.b. Brad Dillingham. How can you be heartbroken over a man like that?"

No point in saying that it was not her heart, but her self-respect, which was still broken. "Thanks, Eileen. See you tomorrow."

When she had hung up, she hesitated for a moment, and then dialed a Cleveland number. Muffy herself, and not her housekeeper of the past fifteen years, answered the phone.

"I got your letter," Joan said. "It's wonderfully kind of you, and I'd love to go."

"Oh, Joaney! I'm so glad."

Joan could picture her—the crop of short gray curls, the blue eyes behind harlequin glasses, the short, plump body encased in some sort of print dress—there in the living room of her Cleveland house.

When Joan last had seen that living room, three years previously, it still had the decor of the early twenties, when Muffy had moved there as the bride of a young state legislator. Joan recalled seeing even a standing lamp with a fringed shade of rose-colored silk, and an upright piano.

"I'll pick you up in New York on the twenty-third. I realize that's only four days from now, but—"

"I'll be ready."

"Wonderful. And come to think of it, I don't see how it will be dull for you," Muffy rushed on, "not with two young men along. Well, I suppose the Frenchman isn't what you'd consider young. Near forty, the Harrises said. But Mr. Manchester's only about thirty. He paid

4

me a visit—you know, to make more arrangements—right after I mailed that letter to you. I told him you might be along. He's awfully nice, and terribly good-looking. And he's a bachelor."

There had been a tentative note in those last few words. Not for the first time, Joan wondered if her elderly relative was quite as naive as everyone thought. Perhaps, even though she had met him only that once the previous summer, Muffy had guessed the truth about Brad.

The meeting had come about entirely by chance. As always during her New York visits, Muffy had wanted to shop, although for her shopping meant admiring the clothes displayed in the stores and then deciding, nine times out of ten, that she didn't need anything. That afternoon they had just emerged, empty-handed, from Saks when Joan saw, with a quickening of her heartbeats, that Brad was walking toward them.

She had introduced him as "the accountant who advised me about Grandmother's estate." They had chatted for a few moments, and then Brad had excused himself, saying that he wanted to get to Brentano's before closing time to pick up a chess book for his son's birthday.

When he came to her apartment late that night, long after Muffy had gone to her hotel, Joan and Brad had agreed that in her cousin's eyes they must have appeared, not lovers, but business acquaintances. Now Joan was not so sure.

"Your Mr. Manchester sounds very nice," she said.

They talked for a few minutes more. Then Joan hung up, walked to the window, and looked down into the back yard of an apartment house facing on Seventy-sixth Street. The March twilight was thickening now, but

5

even so she could see that the branches of the willow tree down there had taken on the yellow tinge of early spring.

The sight of it reminded her of the first afternoon when she and Brad Dillingham had stood at this window, looking down at the tree, that afternoon when she could have said no, I will not go to dinner with you, but instead had said yes.

Abruptly she turned away from the window. She had no time now to think of Brad, thank God. She must think about packing, shopping, and buying traveler's checks, so that in four days' time she would be ready to fly to Paris.

Chapter 2

Paul Lescaut was awakened by the shrilling of the phone on the cigarette-scarred stand beside his bed. He lifted the instrument from its cradle. "Hello."

"May I speak to Etienne Giscard?"

Paul hesitated. Why was he being called again so soon? Less than two months ago, in that small Left Bank café with its noisy pinball machine, he had been paid his semi-annual stipend of ten thousand francs.

"Etienne Giscard speaking," Paul said.

"This is Millard."

The hell it is, Paul thought. This man's voice was deeper than that of the man Paul knew as Millard, and he spoke French with a more pronounced foreign accent.

"What do you want?"

"Meet me in an hour. The usual place." He hung up.

Paul got out of bed and moved across the bare floor to the window. In the gray morning light the room looked as neat, and as cheerless, as an army barracks. He had rented the one-room-kitchenette apartment furnished. Except that he had bought a small, rectangular dining table of unpainted wood to replace one with rickety legs, he had neither added to nor subtracted from the room's furniture, liberally scarred by the cigarettes of some careless former tenant.

At the window he looked down at the slicker-clad

street cleaners, plying their wicker brooms in the gutters. Even at seven in the morning, a few work-bound Parisians hurried along the narrow sidewalk, black umbrellas raised. Paul did not mind that it was raining. For the last eleven years he had minded almost nothing except the occasional lack of money.

He crossed to the small bathroom and turned on the dangling light bulb. He shaved, looking at but not really seeing his mirrored face—the rough blond hair mixed with gray, so that it appeared lighter than it had five years before, the expressionless gray eyes, the nose that was a little thick across the saddle because he had broken it in a long-ago soccer game, the wide, controlled-looking mouth.

He felt only a faint curiosity about what this new Millard wanted of him. As much as possible, he avoided feeling anything. Above all, he avoided thinking of the past, because any chain of memories inevitably led him to Mai and Lisa.

For the same reason, he avoided certain kinds of reading. At the Sorbonne, nearly twenty years before, he had developed a taste for the English metaphysical poets, particularly Donne and Herbert. He no longer read poetry of any kind. He read newspapers, of course, and almost all newly published books on European travel, since he had to be at least as knowledgeable as any of his clients about newly discovered Etruscan tombs or newly established health spas on the Dalmatian coast. He also read histories of earlier centuries, but not the twentieth.

When he had finished shaving, he dressed in a gray suit and a turtleneck sweater of lighter gray. In the closet-sized kitchen, he brewed coffee, and then carried his cup and a plate of croissants to the unpainted table against one wall of his living-dining-bedroom.

Forty minutes later he walked into the narrow café off the Boulevard St. Germain. Even at this early hour, there were four youths gathered around the pinball machine, and the radio behind the counter blared acid rock. At the counter he ordered coffee and then went back along the line of booths. They were all empty, including the last one.

In the past when summoned here, he always had found the man he knew as Millard already seated in the last booth, reading a newspaper. To Paul's faint amusement, usually the paper had been the conservative *Le Figaro*. After a few minutes Millard would fold his newspaper, lay it on the table, and nod farewell. Paul would return the nod, knowing that inside the folded newspaper he would find an envelope holding well-worn thousand-franc notes. Sometimes, although not always, there was also a smaller envelope, bearing a name and some address in Frankfort or Amsterdam or London.

Now he sat down in the last booth. The proprietor's son, a pale, sullen boy of about seventeen, served him coffee and then rejoined the group around the pinball machine. Minutes later a man of about forty-five, with heavy shoulders, unruly eyebrows, and brown hair cut *en brosse*, slid into the opposite side of the booth. He said, his voice barely audible through the rock music and machine-gun clicks of the pinball table, "I'm Millard."

Paul did not bother to contradict him. The other Millard had been older, thinner, and almost ascetic in appearance, with longish hair and with tired-looking hazel eyes behind rimless glasses. He asked, "What is it?"

The sullen youth was approaching, a coffee cup in his hand. Millard waited until the boy had served him the coffee and walked away. Then he said, "You have a client arriving on the twenty-fourth."

9

"Yes."

"We want her."

Paul felt a moment of utter incredulity. "Why? Do you think the old lady is carrying plans for the latest nuclear submarine around in her head?"

"You don't need to know why. All you need to know is that she won't be harmed, In fact, she will be treated as an honored guest."

"Does the other Millard know of your intention to make her your guest?"

"You are not to ask questions." A flicker of expression had crossed the broad face. It made Paul wonder if some sort of accident had been arranged for the other Millard.

A bit of in-fighting among the boys in the Kremlin? Perhaps. But Paul was certain of one thing. Whatever the man across the table and his friends were up to, they had convinced themselves they were doing it for the benefit of their country and perhaps mankind. All the bastards in power all over the world spread suffering and death from the noblest of motives. Paul reflected that probably Genghis Khan, heaping up a new mound of skulls, felt that he was making the world a better as well as a less-crowded place.

As for the three men who killed Mai and Lisa, perhaps they believed that they were enlisted in the most noble cause of all, so noble that raping a young woman and then murdering her and her small daughter was a forgivable peccadillo.

His heart had begun to pound. Stop it. Blot the memory out. He had to keep his mind clear.

The other man asked, "What is your itinerary?"

They must know that already. His prospective client had made a transatlantic call several days before to his cubbyhole office near the Place de l'Opera, and he had

10

been sure for several years now that his telephone was tapped. "I'm to drive her to Florence by way of Geneva," he said. "I have arranged the rental of a villa outside Florence for two weeks. After that she wants to see Venice. She told me she had not made up her mind as to where she would go after that."

"It will be your task to make up her mind for her. After Venice, she will want to drive through the Austrian Alps."

Paul said in a flat voice, "I won't do it."

The other man's tone was mild. "After the free ride you've had for all these years?"

Paul said nothing. Several times he had suspected that it was indeed a free ride, that the envelopes he delivered —always in cities on the itinerary of whatever client he was escorting at the time—had held nothing of importance. They had been keeping him on retainer, so to speak, until they had some real use for him. So much he had guessed, but not that they would demand a kidnaping.

The new Millard said, still in that mild tone, "You haven't developed a love for the Americans, have you?"

If Paul had ever doubted that they knew his past history, that doubt was gone now. They must have known it before the first Millard, representing himself as a prospective client, had walked into his office that spring day almost ten years before. He said, in a hard voice, "Whatever I feel about America or any other country is beside the point. I've got no quarrel with that old lady."

"You're in our pay, and so your quarrels are our quarrels."

"Only up to a certain point. Helping you kidnap a client is beyond that point."

"You made no such stipulation when you made your

agreement with us."

At that time, Paul had been working on his own for only a few months. He had been in the courier business off and on, though, for almost twenty years. While at the Sorbonne, he had worked with his uncle's courier service during summer vacations. After Mai and Lisa's deaths, he had returned to Paris and gone into partnership with his uncle. Only a few months later, the small Cessna his uncle had kept in a private hangar outside Paris had crashed in a vineyard near Reims, killing him instantly.

Paul said, "I have a question. Did some of you boys sabotage my uncle's plane?"

"I am not here to listen to jokes."

"It wasn't a joke. But let that pass. After you make my client your honored guest, what will become of me? Will I also be your guest? Or will I be left for the Austrian police to pick up? Or will you take the simplest course, and shoot me?"

He sounded calm. But his heart was pounding again, not so much with fear, as with anger, including anger at himself. He of all people should have known it was best to steer clear of the Millards of the world, and the shadowy warfare they carried on even in times of so-called peace. Instead he had succumbed to the temptation, not really of the money, but the chance to even a personal score.

"Trust us," Millard said.

"Do I have a choice?"

"Yes. You could try to go to the police, or to your client's embassy. You would be killed before you could enter the building, of course. From now on you will be under continuous observation. True, you could phone from your apartment or office, but we would know about that. Perhaps that way you could save your client inconvenience, but is that worth the cost of your life?"

Paul said nothing. After a moment the other man added, "Don't try to use a public phone for any reason, and stay away from post offices and letter boxes."

Again Paul said nothing.

"And just in case you still feel tempted to go to the authorities," Millard went on, "here is another point for you to ponder. You French are a legalistic race. Your government would be pleased that you had informed upon us, but that would not erase the fact that for ten years you have been in Russian pay. You would go to prison for at least a time, and prison is a dangerous place for a turncoat. It is so easy for his enemies to get at him. After all, anyone can manage to be sent to prison.

"And so you will cooperate. I will not give you the details now, but you will come out of this with your reputation unharmed and your bank account a bit fatter." For the first time since he had been sitting there, he smiled. "We will continue to need the services of an international courier."

Was he, Paul wondered, telling the truth? Perhaps. Probably not, but perhaps.

"The Secret Service man she will have with her," Paul said. "What are your plans for him? And the guards around the villa in Florence. I am sure the American Secret Service will have arranged for a couple of retired *carabinneri* to guard the villa around the clock. What about them?"

"Never mind all that. Just meet your client and drive her to Florence. We will be in touch with you from time to time."

Paul looked with hatred at the man opposite him. One of the few emotions he had allowed himself was pride in how well he did his job. And now—

Well, it could not be helped. He certainly was not going to risk martyrdom for the sake of an elderly widow, especially not this particular widow.

"All right," he said.

⚜

Chapter 3

Even before the movie shown to the handful of first-class passengers was over, Muffy had retired for the night. Short body stretched to almost its full length, she lay across two wide seats, covered by a dark blue blanket.

Across the aisle, Joan was wide awake. The watch strapped to her thin wrist, already set to Paris time, showed almost two in the morning. This would not do. Perhaps a drink would help her get at least a few hours' sleep before the plane landed.

As she moved out into the aisle, she glanced at Dan Manchester in the aisle seat behind Muffy, earphones clamped to his head. He smiled at her. She returned the smile, walked past two sleeping passengers, and climbed the curving stairs to the bar lounge. The plane's two remaining first-class passengers, a fiftyish-looking couple, sat on the beige-upholstered settee nearest the bar. Joan chose the settee beside the lounge entrance, and asked the steward to bring her a vodka and tonic.

She had consumed less than half of her drink when Dan Manchester climbed the stairs and stood smiling down at her. When Muffy had introduced them at Kennedy Airport the evening before, she had been surprised by his looks. Unconsciously she had been expecting a crew-cut, grim-mouthed, pre-Watergate Haldeman type, like the bodyguard she had seen at Muffy's Cleveland house three years before. Instead his hair was brown and curly and moderately long at the neck, his blue eyes and his skin healthy-looking, his smile frequent. If she hadn't known what he was, Joan might have guessed him to be an amateur tennis champion. He said, "Mind if I join you?"

She hesitated and then said, "No, of course not."

He placed the small flight bag he carried on the low table and sat down beside her. "A Scotch and soda, please," he said to the hovering steward. When the man had walked back to the bar, Dan said, "Since we're going to travel together for the next month, I thought we should start getting acquainted."

A smile was her only answer.

Gorgeous girl, he thought. Marvelous eyes, superb legs. But she was jumpy as a gazelle. He had seen her shoulders tense the moment he had entered the lounge. What was she afraid of? Men?

The steward set the drink down, withdrew. She asked, "What's in the flight bag?"

"A gun. Want to see it?"

"No, thanks." She went on, with the air of one making conversation, "Do you like your job?"

"It's all right. A little dull most of the time."

"Dull!"

"Oh, the Secret Service doesn't overthrow foreign governments or compile dossiers on Congressmen's love lives. We leave that to the other branches of the service." He smiled to make it clear that he was joking. "We're just glorified guard dogs." He added, "But when I said my job was dull, I didn't mean this trip."

She ignored that. "I've been wondering about your name. Are you any relation to *the* Daniel Manchester?"

"He's my father."

"Really?"

"Yes, that's my old man. The John Wayne of American industry. Founder of the Save America League." He looked at her with mock anxiety. "You're not one of those liberal types who spit three times whenever they hear his name, are you?"

"No. I'm nothing. Politics has never turned me on."

"I've been wondering about that. What does turn you on?"

After a moment she said, "Right now? The thought of getting a few hours' sleep. That's why I ordered this drink."

He accepted her refusal of his gambit. "Your cousin's already asleep. Is she your mother's cousin?"

"My grandmother's."

"Well, she's a very nice person. She's another reason I'm glad I asked for this assignment."

Again she ignored the implied compliment. "You asked for it?"

"Yes. I liked the idea of a European trip. And I admired your cousin's husband." He laughed. "So did my old man, although he would never admit it. Wrong party, you know."

"I suppose so." She took a final swallow of her drink and stood up. "Well, good night."

"Good night."

She went down the stairs and sat down in the window seat she had left fifteen minutes before. Dan Manchester, she thought. He was young, single, and handsome, and had a secure and probably well-paid job. And because of her present state, he was completely wasted on her.

She was sure that he would not have been wasted two years ago, before she met Brad Dillingham.

Ironically it was her boss, now his most vituperative

critic, who had brought her and Brad together. If she needed advice about the stocks her grandmother had left her, Eileen Haskel had said Dillingham was the man to call. "He's a CPA and an investment counselor, and since he's done some accounting for the magazine from time to time, he won't charge you an arm and a leg."

"I should hope not," Joan had said. "It's what you would call a very modest estate."

Modest, but complicated. Joan's grandmother had taken to heart that frequently heard advice about diversifying one's portfolio. At her death she had owned one municipal bond in each of a half-dozen cities, and a few shares of stock, sometimes only one share, in almost fifty companies.

The next Saturday afternoon Joan had opened her door and seen Brad for the first time. She judged his age to be about thirty-five. He was a tall man—half a head taller than her own height of five-feet-seven inches—with dark hair, warm gray eyes behind horn-rimmed glasses, and a mobile-looking mouth with a full underlip. Even as he said, "Miss Creighton? I'm Bradford Dillingham," she was aware of the current of attraction flowing between them.

But before more than a few minutes had passed, she knew that she had no excuse not to ignore that attraction. By then he had let her know that he was married. Looking at her row of Japanese prints, he had remarked casually that his wife Sheila had bought similar prints at a recent auction. Seated beside her on the sofa, with the lists of Grandmother Creighton's investments spread out before him on the coffee table, he had said that a certain pharmaceutical company was a particularly good investment. In fact, he had just put aside shares in that company for his kids. Nancy was twelve, he told her, in answer to her question, and Jimmy was almost eleven.

He went down the list, writing beside each stock its current value, and checking those which he thought she should sell. At last he said, glancing at his watch, "Almost five. We haven't quite finished, but maybe we'd better put it off until some afternoon next week. You have copies of these lists, don't you?"

She nodded.

"Then I'll take these along with me."

He placed the papers in his briefcase. They both rose. Then, instead of moving toward the door, he crossed to the window and stood looking down. Joan moved to his side.

"Whenever I see a willow tree," he said, "I think of a place I wanted to buy years ago in northern Connecticut, near a little town called West Amnity. It had twenty acres, an apple orchard, and a hundred-and-fifty-year-old house with a porch running along two sides. It also had a pond surrounded with weeping willows."

"Northern Connecticut sounds pretty far away for commuting."

"I wanted to give up New York entirely, and hang out my shingle in West Amnity. I'd have been the only CPA for miles around. And if I could have gotten that orchard back in shape, it might have made a little money."

She pictured apple trees covered with pink-and-white blossoms, and willow branches trailing in a pond's still waters. "Why didn't you do it? It sounds like a wonderful life."

He turned his head and looked down at her. Again she was aware of that pull of attraction. "Oh, it didn't work out, for several reasons, and now it's too late." He went on looking at her, gray eyes somber now. Then he said with a rush. "No point in waiting until next week. We

19

could clean up those few details over dinner. I know this quiet little Italian place a couple of blocks from here."

She waited until she was sure her tone would be matter-of-fact. "But doesn't your wife expect you home for dinner?"

"No. You see, my wife and I have an—understanding. We're only waiting until the kids—" He broke off abruptly, and then said, "No, she doesn't expect me. I'm staying in town tonight so that tomorrow I can play golf on Long Island with an important customer. I often stay in town weekends for business reasons. If I don't have dinner with you tonight, I'll have it alone. So we might as well go over those last few stocks."

Yes, better to finish the matter. But even as the thought formed, she knew she was deceiving herself. "I'd like to change," she said, "if you don't mind waiting. You'll find the makings in the kitchen, if you want to fix yourself a drink."

In the Italian restaurant they did go over the other securities on her list. But they also talked of other matters. It was his wife's opposition which, in the second year of their marriage, had made the dream of that old farmhouse and apple orchard impossible. She had preferred Westchester. And so he had buckled down to his job with a Manhattan firm so arduously that now he was one of the company's three vice-presidents.

For a while he had grown dwarf apple trees on his less-than-an-acre in Westchester. But as the children grew older they had wanted what many of their friends had, a swimming pool and a tennis court, and so, to make room, he had uprooted his trees.

In his wallet he had a half-dozen snapshots of his children, a thin, pretty blond girl and a boy, also blond, who was engagingly gap-toothed in the earlier photos. His wife Sheila was in two of the snapshots. In both she was casually but smartly dressed in a pants suit, an attractive, slightly overweight woman with a self-assured face framed in dark blond hair.

Joan carried no snapshots, but she did tell him a little about herself. Her uneventful childhood in a small Indiana town. Her four years at Barnard, and her first and only job at *Today's Woman*. She had started out as a typist-reader. It was partly because the staff was so small that she had been able to advance rapidly to an assistant editorship, with occasional writing assignments on the side.

Around eleven they parted at her apartment door with a decorous handshake. But Joan did not sleep well that night. And two days later, at the office, she was not surprised to receive a phone call from him. He would like to change his recommendation about some of those stocks. Perhaps they could talk about it over dinner—

It was not until the fourth of those dinners in small, quiet restaurants that he spoke the words which, it seemed to Joan, had been inevitable since the moment they met. By that time she was thoroughly in love. Each time her phone rang, either in the apartment or at the office, her heart quickened. Often at work she realized, with a start, that she had stared out of the window for perhaps ten minutes, while an unedited manuscript lay on her desk. Once Eileen, watching her with amused eyes, asked, "Is it that serious?"

"Yes. But I don't want to talk about it." If she did, her cynical boss would tell her she was a fool. Eileen knew nothing of the "understanding" between Brad and his wife, nothing of the blasted dream about the small-town office, and the again-flourishing apple orchard, and the pond reflecting willows.

Near the end of that fourth dinner, in that Italian

21

restaurant where they first had faced each other across a table, he set down his coffee cup and said abruptly, "I have to talk to you."

She waited, the pulse in her throat beating hard.

"I suppose you've gathered that my marriage has been dead for a long, long time. Sheila and I have not touched each other in years, and never will again. Whether or not there have been other men in Sheila's life I don't know. I don't know whether she knows about my few brief flings, but if she does, I'm sure she doesn't care.

"A couple of years from now the kids will both be in their teens. You know how teen-agers are. These days they have almost a complete life of their own. And they're bright kids. I think they've already guessed that Sheila and I are headed for the divorce court. But even if they haven't guessed—well, it won't be the shock to them it would have been earlier."

He paused, and then went on, "That place in Connecticut. There's not much chance it's for sale now. But there are other places. You like the idea, don't you? You couldn't very well commute to New York. But you could still write, couldn't you?"

She said through a tightened throat, "Brad, I don't understand exactly what—"

He groaned. "Of course you don't. I've been thinking about this for days, and now I'm saying it all wrong. What I should have said first is that I love you. I don't think that comes as any news to you, does it?"

Smiling, unable to speak, she shook her head.

"Then you'll marry me the moment I'm free?"

"Of course I will."

She saw the leap of joy in his eyes. "Let's get out of here," he said.

It was a Tuesday night. Only a few people sat at the

small tables, and all of them were intent upon their food or each other. As Brad helped her on with her coat, he bent and kissed the crown of her head, the first of many times he was to do that.

His hands gripped her shoulders. "Please don't send me away tonight. Please don't."

The pressure of his hands sent a wave of warmth down her body. Neither she nor Brad was extremely young any more. And two years was a long time to wait. "I won't send you away," she said.

For nearly a year and a half, she had been happy. True, there were occasional lonely and disappointing evenings and weekends, when Brad called to say he could not be with her after all. Sometimes it was work that kept him away. Other times it was his daughter's school play, or his son's Little League playoff game. One weekend it was an unexpected visit from his parents in upstate New York.

But other times more than made up for the lonely hours. Several weekends they house-hunted through Connecticut, upper New York State, and even New Hampshire, driving between fields that first were filled with cabbages, blossoming potatoes, and wind-stirred rows of corn, then brown and stubbly after harvesttime, then emerald with winter wheat, and then, as spring and summer rolled around, again filled with row upon row of burgeoning plants.

His dream farm was lost to them. They parked one afternoon on a hillside and looked down at the house. A man with a wheelbarrow moved between rows of fruit-laden trees, picking up fallen apples. A woman on the veranda that ran along two sides of the house beat a small blue rug which hung over the railing. Two boys of about nine and seven, each with a toy sailboat in hand, moved toward the willow-bordered pond.

23

But they found other places that were for sale, none of them perfect, each with possibilities. Before falling asleep in some motel room or country inn, they would lie in each other's arms and drowsily debate the merits of a hilltop house with little land against those of another house with thirty acres but no view.

Early in November, about eighteen months after they had met, it was Joan who had to cancel their weekend arrangements. During midafternoon coffee break she called his office and told him that Eileen wanted her to go to Baltimore the next day to tape an interview with an aged suffragette leader. His voice had echoed her own disappointment.

That disappointment turned to sharp annoyance when Eileen called her at her apartment that night. The interview was off. The suffragette's nurse-companion had called to say that the elderly woman was ill. By then it was too late to salvage the weekend. She had never called Brad at his Westchester house, and never would.

She would have welcomed a rainy Saturday. Instead it turned out to be one of those November days that seem to be a leftover from the Indian summer just past, or a preview of the distant spring.

Thinking it might make her feel less lonely, toward one o'clock she put a paperback book in her purse, walked three blocks to Central Park, and took a path leading to a refreshment stand. Several times she and Brad had lunched there. On chilly days they had eaten cheese sandwiches or wizened hot dogs inside the little restaurant. On other days they had carried their food out to the tables on the porch overlooking the lake.

When she entered the little place, one glance through the broad windows along the rear wall told her that all the tables out on the porch were taken. At the counter she ordered a cheese sandwich and a container of coffee, and then carried her food over to an empty table beside a window.

She took a sip of coffee, opened her book, and picked up her sandwich. It was then that she heard Brad's hearty laugh. Her head lifted, and then turned toward the window. He sat at a table out there, back turned to her. His pretty blond daughter, Nancy, was on his right, his son Jimmy on his left. Sheila sat opposite him, a little plumper than in those snapshots, and still smiling at whatever it was—probably a sally from one of the kids —which had provoked Brad's laughter.

Joan told herself that there was no reason for this wrenching jealousy, no reason why, under the circumstances, that Brad should not take his children to spend this beautiful day in Central Park. Nor was there any reason why the children's mother should not join the party.

Still, she herself must get out of here right away. Sheila's paper plate was empty. Only an inch or so of Nancy's pinkish milkshake remained in its tall glass. Soon they would be coming back through the restaurant. But she still sat there, staring at the blond woman who for fifteen years had been Mrs. Bradford Dillingham.

Sheila pushed her chair back. Brad got to his feet and circled the table. Before he helped Sheila to rise—she seemed to be having a little difficulty—he bent and kissed the top of her head.

As Joan sat there, frozen, Sheila got to her feet. Now it was apparent why her movements were awkward. She was about eight months pregnant.

It was not until the four of them walked toward the doorway that Joan herself was able to move. Stomach churning, she got to her feet and hurried toward the ladies' room. When she finally emerged, the Dillinghams were nowhere in sight.

On Monday, Brad called her at her office. Without even thinking about it, she hung up the instant she heard his voice. Then she lifted the phone and asked the switchboard operator, "Would you recognize the voice of the man who just called me?"

"Yes." Her tone added, "Why shouldn't I, after a year and a half?"

"If he calls again, don't put him through. Tell him I'll be out of the office all day."

She replaced the phone and looked up. Her boss stood in the doorway. "You look as if someone had been feeding you arsenic," Eileen said. "Better come into my office and get it out of your system right away."

In Eileen's office, Joan told the whole story. In a quiet voice, Eileen called Brad Dillingham a few of the names that angry truck drivers hurl at each other. Then she said, "Welcome to the club, baby."

Joan felt dull surprise. "You mean you were ever foolish enough to—"

"I was. We really ought to form a club, you know, all of us women who've believed that I'll-get-a-divorce-when-the-kids-are-a-little-older line. Our club pin could be a small sterling silver dunce cap. Now go home, but be here at nine sharp tomorrow. Work's the best cure for anything."

That evening her apartment phone rang three times between seven and eight. She let it ring. After a while the downstairs buzzer sounded. She ignored it. Then, apparently, he used the old trick of pushing several apartment buttons for admittance, because soon he was at her door, ringing the bell.

She crossed the room, fastened the burglar chain, and

opened the door a few inches. Plainly he had not guessed what she knew because his face, although alarmed, held no guilt. "Joan, what is it, darling? What's the matter?"

She felt that churning sensation in her stomach again. She said rapidly, "I was at the refreshment stand in the park Saturday. I saw your wife."

Consternation in his eyes now. His face went red, then pale. He said, "Oh, God! I know what you must have felt. Let me in. Let me talk to you about it."

She did not want to go on looking at him, but there was at least one thing that had to be said. "Talk? What can you possibly say about that lie you told me? Your marriage was dead, you said, for now and forever."

He had nothing to say, at least nothing he could hope would make the situation any better. The guilty bafflement in his eyes told her that. He reached his hand past the edge of the door. "Joan, if you'll just let me in—"

She took a step backward. "Don't try to touch me. If you touched me, I'd be sick right here. Take your hand away. And never come near me again."

He withdrew his hand. She had a last glimpse of his bleak face before she closed the door and locked it.

Evidently he had been convinced that she meant every word she said, because after that he had never tried to see her or even talk to her on the phone.

Many times she had wondered if he were what Eileen believed him to be, a ruthless sexual exploiter. Or was he, despite his comparative success, a man who had never grown up enough to achieve emotional commitment? Perhaps he had alternated between two men, one of them Sheila's occasionally bored but on the whole not too unhappy husband, the other a man who told himself that someday he would realize, with Joan, his youthful dream of the small-town office and the flourishing apple farm.

27

Well, she would never know the truth about that.

Now she turned and looked across the plane's aisle at her kinswoman. Muffy was sound asleep, gray curls encased in a blue scarf, lips slightly parted. Her gentle snoring was audible through the muted roar of the jets.

Had any episode in Muffy's life ever left her with a sense, not just of betrayal, but of self-doubt and broken self-esteem? Probably not. She had been the childhood sweetheart of the ferociously ambitious man she called Buzz. Chances were that now she was the only one in the world who thought of him by the family nickname given him as a toddler. His parents and even his siblings were long since dead. It had always been apparent to everyone that he loved the seemingly ordinary woman he had married. If he had been unfaithful to her, he surely had protected her from the fact with the same wiliness he had used in his rise to the heights of power.

Joan turned and looked through the plane's window. The moon had set now. Below the huge wing an undulating sea of clouds shone faintly in the starlight. She really must try to get some sleep. Soon it would be dawn. She curled up on the two seats and drew a blanket up around her shoulders.

Dan Manchester paused at the foot of the lounge stairs long enough to look at her. Eyelids hid the marvelous eyes, and a blanket covered the superb legs and the too-thin but beautifully proportioned body.

Sometimes it was hard for a man to keep his mind on his job. But he had better, particularly this job. He walked down the aisle to his seat.

Chapter 4

A minute or so after the waiting room loud-speaker at Charles de Gaulle Airport announced the arrival of the New York jet, Paul Lescaut extinguished his cigarette in a sand-filled urn, got to his feet, and took up his station just beyond the customs desk. His rough blond head, usually bare to the weather, was now covered by a black beret. Like many couriers, he had chosen a beret as a suitable compromise between the conventional headgear worn by his male clients and the visored cap of someone whose sole duty was driving.

He held in front of his chest a piece of cardboard about a foot square, with his client's name hand-lettered upon it. It was a common name, and elicited no second glances from others waiting to greet arriving passengers. Above the cardboard his face had assumed its professional mask —alert, pleasant, but touched with deference. It was an expression designed to keep at arm's length any client bent upon fraternizing.

He decided that he would not have long to wait. Passengers from other flights were moving rapidly through the immigration line—several Japanese, two Englishmen, and a German family. He automatically ticked off their nationalities as they answered the custom inspector's questions and then came through the little gate. Long ago he had learned to differentiate at sight Americans from Europeans, and various European nationals from each other, even when the French or Italian or American men had patronized Saville Row tailors, and the German or Portuguese or English women had bought their clothes from Paris couturiers. Whenever he had been able to check his assumptions, invariably they had proved to be correct.

A number of Americans, probably first-class passengers from the New York flight, had joined the line now. His gaze swept over them. Which one? That tall, heavy woman with the hennaed hair and the blond mink coat pushed carelessly back from her shoulders? No, she was too young by at least twenty years, and the stout, gray-haired man behind her probably was her husband. Certainly he was not a Secret Service man.

The line moved forward. A short woman behind the gray-haired man came into view. Catching sight of Lescaut's sign, she smiled and waved.

He felt surprise. Perhaps he had seen a picture of her at some time in the past. If so, he had forgotten it. He had expected someone more imposing, certainly not that plump little creature in an outmoded gray Persian lamb coat which made her look even plumper. But he was certain she was the one, not just because of the wave and smile, but also because of the tall man behind her. Over the years, shepherding VIP's around Europe, Lescaut had acquired some experience with bodyguards, both private ones and those from various governmental agencies. This one had his profession written all over him. And he looked intelligent and extremely fit. Lescaut reflected grimly that Millard and his friends had best not underestimate the widow's companion.

The little woman and the tall young man were walking toward him now. Somewhere Lescaut had read the observation that European men walk cautiously, Englishmen walk as if they owned the earth, and Americans walk as if they didn't care who owned it. That was the way this man walked, with a free, confident stride. In his right hand he carried a flight bag. His gun, probably a thirty-eight revolver, would be in that. In his left he carried a large tapestry tote bag. That would be the client's.

Then Lescaut saw the girl walking a pace or two behind the old lady, a tall girl with a thin, tired-looking face, and a cap of dark red hair that covered her ears and fanned out on her cheeks. Her greenish-gray eyes were almost the same shade as the tweed coat she wore over a darker green sweater and skirt. Surely she was not with the other two. She must be a fellow passenger to whom they had promised a lift to her hotel.

"So you're Mr. Lescaut." His client extended her hand. It felt as soft and almost as small was a child's. "This is Mr. Manchester. And this— Joan? Where are— Oh, there you are. This is my cousin, Miss Creighton. She's coming with us. On the tour, I mean. Maybe I should have let you know, but it was all sort of last-minutey. I hope it won't mean extra trouble for you."

He felt a tightness across his chest. Did Millard's people know she was coming? And what would they do about her?

"No trouble at all, madame. How do you do, Miss Creighton, Mr. Manchester."

He collected their luggage and, with the three of them trailing behind him, followed two baggage porters through hazy sunlight out to the parking lot. Before he opened the rear door of the tan Mercedes, he said, "This is my own car, madame. Before we leave Paris tomorrow, I can lease a Rolls town car, if you would prefer it."

"Oh, heavens no! I'll want to ask you questions as we go along, and I hate talking through one of those tubes." She paused. "You are a careful driver, aren't you? I don't like to go over fifty miles an hour."

"With a client in the car, madame, I never drive over fifty."

He ushered the two women into the rear seat. Manchester asked, "Okay if I ride up front with you?"

"Whatever you like, sir."

Manchester smiled. "You can skip the sir. I'm not a client. The government's picking up my tab."

The outgoing kind, Lescaut thought, as the American placed the flight bag between them on the front seat. Soon he would suggest that they use first names. Soon after that the questions would start. Married? Ever been married? Lescaut always answered "no" to both questions, so flatly that the questioner almost invariably dropped the subject. Still, he disliked the well-intentioned curiosity of others, and now, with anxiety weighing upon him, he disliked the prospect of it even more.

As they drove between brown, newly plowed fields, Manchester asked, "You like this line of work?"

Paul gave his usual answer. "Yes, I've always liked to travel."

"Your clients ever get in your hair?"

There was also a standard answer to that. "If there are two couples, sometimes one will want to vary the itinerary—with a side trip to North Africa, say—and the other will want to keep to the original arrangement. Then there's trouble. Otherwise things go very smoothly."

"You must speak several languages."

"A few. French, of course. I learned English in school. My Italian and German are fair, and I know enough Hungarian, Yugoslav and Czech to get through border

32

formalities and engage hotel rooms, and so on."

"You take clients to eastern Europe?"

"If they want me to."

"Ever have any trouble there?"

Lescaut cursed himself. Nerve strain had made him unguarded. He need not have named all the languages he spoke. With such an opening, Manchester might want to talk Cold War politics from now on.

"I always make sure that mine and my clients' papers are in order, and I am especially careful to obey all traffic laws when in eastern Europe. So far I have had no trouble."

"You're lucky. Those boys behind the Iron Curtain play really rough."

They came to three miles of road under construction. As if he realized that Lescaut must give all his attention to the traffic, narrowing from three lanes to two and then one, Manchester fell silent. Now and then Lescaut took a quick look in the broad rear-view mirror at the girl. Apparently she'd had insufficient sleep on the plane. She sat in one corner of the seat with her eyes closed, brown lashes fanned out on her white cheeks. Each time he looked at her he felt a fresh surge of anger. And it was not, he realized, just because her presence added further complication to a dilemma that already threatened his livelihood and even his life. There was still another reason, one he could not define, why he wished that she had stayed on her side of the Atlantic.

One thing he was sure of. Even though her elderly cousin might be rich—and probably was, in spite of that old-fashioned fur coat—the girl was not. He'd had enough experience to recognize the differences between the born-rich and the new-rich, and both types from those to whom a weekly pay check was important.

He wondered what her voice was like. As yet he had not heard her speak. When introduced, she had only smiled and nodded.

The bad stretch of road was behind them now. In the distance he could see Sacré-Coeur on its high bluff, its dome gleaming in the sunlight. He said, "Will this be your first visit to Paris, madame?"

"Oh, no. I was here twice before with my husband. He was only a Congressman then. We were on junkets. Maybe you don't know that word. It sounds like something to eat. But it means a trip that Congressmen take."

The girl's eyes were open now. "I know, madame," Lescaut said. "And you, miss? Is this your first time in Europe?"

"No. I was here one summer while I was in college."

Her voice was low and well modulated, but there was a deadness at the center of it. Fatigue? Something more than that?

They were in the city now. Lescaut divided his attention between the always tricky Paris traffic and Manchester, who was comparing the merits of the Mercedes with those of the English Bentley and the American Cadillac. Then, when he stopped at a traffic signal on Boulevard des Italiens, Lescaut saw the display in a travel agency's window. A three-foot-high replica of a Buddhist pagoda, and a blownup color photograph of men in wide conical hats, with carrying poles balanced across their shoulders. It brought him a childhood memory, a bearable, even pleasant memory.

The cool, shadowy living room of the big plantation house. He sat on the floor, pushing a red toy car across the straw matting. Another car, a real one, passed beyond the long veranda. His father, on his way to his office in Saigon? Some of the plantation workers, driving in a bucket-laden truck toward the stands of rubber trees? He did not know then, or now. His memory had retained just the sound of an engine.

His mother had been in the room, seated in a fan-back wicker chair, her blond hair curving to her shoulders in the long bob of the nineteen-thirties. She wore a pink garment, something he knew were called lounging pajamas, and she sat with one slender leg crossed over the opposite knee, reading one of the fashion magazines sent to her regularly from Paris.

Making a car noise in his throat, he pushed the toy close to her pink, open-toed sandal, drew it back, pushed it forward again until it touched the sandal's sole. "Don't do that, my darling," his mother said, and he answered, "Yes, Mama."

That was the end of the memory. Strange that such an inconsequential one should be his only memory from his first four years of life. But then, probably they had been uneventful, happy years, the sort that do not leave traces in a young child's memory. Certainly his later childhood had been happy.

Through Manchester's comments and his own replies he now and then heard some of the conversation in the back seat. The old lady and the girl were discussing whether they should shop or sight-see during their few hours in Paris.

If only he could get in touch with Millard about the girl. But they had never given him a phone number to call. All he could do was to hope that before he started for Florence tomorrow Millard would call him.

He turned onto the Rue de la Paix, and then stopped

35

in the Place Vendome before an old and world-famous hotel. Inside, he waited until the three of them had registered and were moving toward the elevators in the wake of two baggage-laden bellmen. Then he went out to the Mercedes.

Since there was nothing else he could do, he spent the rest of the day following his usual pre-tour routine. He took the Mercedes to a garage for lubrication and a final tuning of its engine. He made two calls to Geneva, reserving three rooms at a first-class hotel for the two women and Manchester, and a room at a cheaper hotel for himself. He phoned the housekeeper of the rented villa in Florence and told her that there would be three in the party.

Late in the afternoon he made another call to Florence. Carlotta answered the phone. Her two younger children were screaming in the background. It was not until she yelled them into silence that he could make himself understood.

"Could you get my room ready? I'll be in Florence on Thursday."

"Sure, Paolo. How long will you be here this time?"

"Two weeks. How's Giovanni?" Giovanni was her husband, a waiter in one of Florence's best restaurants.

"Giovanni's fine. He says tips are down, though. Is there anything wrong, Paolo? You sound—strange."

"No, nothing wrong. I'll see you Thursday."

He ate without appetite that night in a small restaurant on the Rue de Richelieu, and then walked back to his flat. The moment he had closed the door behind him, the phone rang.

"May I speak to Etienne Giscard?"

"Cut the crap," Lescaut said angrily. The call had been timed, he realized, to let him know how closely he was being watched, probably at the moment from some building across the street. "Do you know the old lady brought a girl with her, some kind of a cousin?"

"We know."

"Why in hell didn't you tell me about her the other day?"

"We didn't know then that she was coming here. Now get hold of yourself. She's an unexpected factor, and one that will have to be eliminated. But that can be managed."

"What do you mean, eliminated?" Lescaut's voice was thick.

"Nothing drastic. She must be persuaded to return to America, that's all."

"That's all. Who's to do the persuading? Me?"

"If so, you'll receive instructions to that effect. Now just do your job."

There was a click. After a moment Paul also hung up. Persuaded. The Millards of the world relied mainly upon one form of persuasion—fear. What did they plan to do to her, that too-thin girl with the dark red hair? He remembered her in the car's rear seat, lashes like brown fans on her pale cheeks.

Suddenly he knew why the first sight of her had shaken him. She reminded him of Mai.

Not that anyone else would perceive the resemblance. Mai had been only five feet tall, and her hair, which reached almost to her waist when she released it from its sleek knot, had been black. But she'd had that same fine-boned delicacy, and her legs, like the Creighton girl's, had been long in proportion to the rest of her.

As sometimes happened, the dam he had erected between himself and the past crumbled, and memories came flooding through. Mai's upturned, laughing face one Saturday when they had stopped at a Seine bookstall to look at a collection of ancient postcards. Mai in the bedroom of their Saigon house, her delicate body shuddering beneath his, her face holding a pleasure so intense it might have been pain. Mai, in a green *ao-dai*, the graceful Vietnamese costume he loved to see her wear, running in simulated terror along the graveled garden path, with their three-year-old daughter behind her, chubby legs pumping, lovely little face gleeful.

So it was to be one of those nights. He went into the kitchen, took down a bottle of Calvados and a glass from the cupboard, and carried them to the bare dining table. He sat down and poured himself what he knew would be the first of several drinks.

They had fallen in love, that spring of 1954, while they were both second-year students at the Sorbonne. It had disturbed them only a little that her family, Vietnamese aristocrats, would be no more pleased than his. They had both felt—rightly, as it turned out—that their families would become reconciled to their marriage. Such alliances between French colonialists and Vietnamese Catholics were not too uncommon in French Indochina.

Paul and Mai were more disturbed, of course, by the warfare raging in what had been her family's homeland for many generations, and his family's adopted home for only a few years before his own birth. At besieged Dien Bien Phu, where attacking Vietnamese soldiers rained constant fire on French soldiers huddled in bunkers, it had become grimly evident that, despite American aid,

French rule of that beautiful tropical land was finished.

But to Paul and Mai, together and in love in spring-time Paris, the prolonged agony at Dien Bien Phu seemed far away. Besides, whatever the post-colonial government, her family would play its traditional role as high civil servants, and his family would maintain its prosperous rubber plantation. And as always, French planters and rich Vietnamese would gather on the terrace of Le Cercle Sportif at cocktail time, and on weekends swim from the beautifully kept beaches at their private clubs.

At the end of that term, Mai had returned to Saigon to plead their case with her parents. Paul, at his Uncle Henri's urgent request, had stayed on in Paris for the summer, escorting rich Americans through the château-dotted Loire Valley and across the border to the flower-strewn upland meadows of the Swiss Alps. When Mai's first letter arrived, he learned that she had been only partially successful. They must wait, her parents insisted, until they both were graduated from the Sorbonne. Because he had hoped that they, like several couples they knew, could marry while still at the university, he had felt sharp disappointment. But better to wait for Mai than not to have her at all. Besides, except in the summertime, they would still be together.

Less than a month after their graduation, he stood in the Saigon Cathedral and watched Mai move toward him down the aisle, so ethereally lovely in a white lace dress and a cap of seed pearls that he, who already considered her the most beautiful woman in the world, felt a kind of disbelieving shock.

They toured the Greek islands on a one-month honeymoon, and then settled down in the small but pleasant house, in a Saigon suburb, which had been her parents' wedding gift to them. With the help of a maid-of-all-work, Mai spent her days keeping house, playing bridge with her Vietnamese and French women friends, and trying out recipes from her growing collection of Vietnamese, French, and Chinese cookbooks. Paul took charge of his father's Saigon office, leaving the elder Lescaut free to devote all his attention to the rubber plantation.

The French soldiers were gone by that time. In Geneva the world's leaders, gathered around a conference table, had decided that temporarily Vietnam would be divided into northern and southern regions, pending free elections that would reunite the country in 1956.

But now it seemed that the election was not to be held, after all. The Saigon regime, declaring the southern part of Vietnam a separate country, had canceled the election. In the north, battle-hardened veterans of the long struggle against the French began to stockpile arms supplied by China and Russia. In the south, like-minded bands of guerrilla fighters began to take over remote villages, burn rubber and rice plantations, and, with their fire bombs, make the roads perilous at night for traveling Saigon officials. But in Saigon itself, that sophisticated city called the Paris of the Orient, life for people like Paul and Mai continued at its usual pleasant, leisurely pace.

By the time Melissa was born, in the fourth year of their marriage, American military advisers were helping Saigon's army in its struggle against the pajama-clad guerrillas who slipped like shadows along the jungle paths from hamlet to hamlet. Over the next few years, United States soldiers arrived in ever-increasing numbers, young men who looked like giants to their Vietnamese allies, and who spent their pay freely in Saigon's restaurants and bars. But despite the Americans moving from hamlet to hamlet, automatic rifles at the ready, more villages came, willingly or unwillingly, under control of the Viet Cong guerrillas, and more cars carrying government officials were blown to bits on the roads around Saigon. And in the city itself bombs exploded in cafés, theaters, and market places.

Lisa was not yet five the day that Paul, at work in his office, heard an explosion nearby. Aware that Mai had arranged to lunch with friends in a restaurant a few doors away, he rushed into the street. Smoke billowed from the café's shattered front windows. In the distance, sirens shrieked.

He was pushing his way frantically through the small crowd which had gathered when someone grasped his arm. He turned to see a business acquaintance, a rubber broker with offices directly opposite the café. "Your wife isn't in there, Lescaut. I saw her and her friends drive off half an hour ago."

Badly shaken, he drove home and told his wife that she and Lisa must leave Saigon.

"Leave?" Her face was bewildered. "Where shall we go?"

"Your uncle and aunt's house."

"But they aren't there!" The week before, Mai's parents and her uncle and aunt had left for a two months' stay with relatives in France.

"They left the servants there."

"Not all of them. They took the two maids with them."

"There's still the gardener and the cook. You'll be safe there. And I'll drive up every weekend."

The house, forty miles from Saigon, was set in the midst of what had once been a rubber plantation. Years ago the trees had begun to succumb to a disease popularly known as leaf-fall. Because he had more than an adequate income from South African gold mining stock, Mai's uncle had let the plantation go back to jungle.

It was a safe area. As far as anyone knew, the Viet Cong had not even tried to infiltrate it, probably because all the nearby villages, influenced by priests who maintained a medical center for them, were staunchly pro-government.

"Every weekend? How long do you expect us to stay away?" Her upturned face held dismayed protest. Mai loved her house, her native city, and her life with him and their daughter and their friends.

"Until Saigon is a safer place for you. If anything happened to you or Lisa, I wouldn't want to live."

The mutiny left her eyes. "All right, my darling. We will go."

He drove her and their little girl to the house the next day, and left them in the care of the middle-aged gardener and woman cook, both of whom had worked for various members of Mai's family all their adult lives. The next three weekends he left an increasingly jittery Saigon and drove to the old plantation house, with its cool, high-ceilinged rooms and its veranda overlooking a semicircular drive and a broad lawn set with scarlet hibiscus bushes.

On the fourth weekend he emerged from the road through the jungle and then braked to a stop, staring in stunned disbelief at what remained of the house. Only the fire-blackened corner posts and the lower portion of an interior staircase still stood. The rest had collapsed into still-smoking ruins.

He got out of the car and ran to a rear corner of the house. The room Mai had chosen had been there, next

43

to the nursery her cousins had occupied as children. Careless of the pain, with his bare hands he thrust two slanted and smoldering beams aside and looked down at the charred rubble. No sign of either of them here, and no sign of them among the ruins of what had been the nursery. They must have escaped in time. Probably the servants had too.

Where had they gone? He stood still for a moment, and then ran across the lawn and plunged into the path that ran through the jungle to the nearest village, half a mile away. At a swift dogtrot he moved through the hot stillness. It was that midday hour when the monkeys and even the noisy parrots are silenced by the heat. Why had the house caught fire? An accident? Viet Cong?

He emerged into the village clearing and then stopped short. Two black-pajamaed men, Viet Cong, lay crumpled on the ground, hands tied behind them. Each had been shot in the back of the head. Near them lay the bullet-ridden body of the middle-aged gardener, and a few yards farther away the body of the plump, gray-haired cook. He looked wildly around him. No sign of anyone else, living or dead.

Calling his wife's name, he ran to the nearest hut and looked inside. No one. Just sleeping mats and a low table and a cooking pot on a charcoal brazier. The next hut, too, was empty.

He found her between the second and third huts. She lay on the ground in a blue *ao-dai*, dark eyes still open, and still holding an expression of incredulous horror. The front of her dress, dyed crimson by blood from a bayonet thrust below her left breast, showed how she had died. That look in her eyes, and the attitude in which her body lay, told him what had happened to her before she died. Too numb to feel anything at all in those first few moments, he knelt, straightened her limbs and pulled her dress down to her ankles, and then closed the lids of those staring eyes.

He got to his feet. Where was his baby? He began to run in one direction and then the other, calling for her.

He found Lisa at the foot of a tree at the clearing's edge. Something, probably a rifle butt, had caved in the back of her dark little head.

For an interval after that he must have been insane. He did not remember carrying Lisa in his arms and placing her beside her mother, but he must have done so, because after a while he became aware that he was on his knees beside both of them, beating the ground with his fists and yelling.

Movement at the other side of the clearing, just beyond the first line of trees. He stood up, dashed across the clearing, and, after a brief chase along a dim path, closed his hands around thin shoulders. His captive was a boy of ten or eleven, clad in ragged blue cotton shorts, and big-eyed with fear.

Crouching so that his face was on a level with the child's, Lescaut said, "What happened here? Tell me!"

The boy just stared at him in terrified silence.

"Who did all this? Tell me!" The boy looked wildly to the right and then the left, as if trying to see whether or not listeners lurked among the trees. Lescaut gave the narrow shoulders a shake. "Tell me!"

The boy whispered, "Viet Cong burned the house, I think."

"Never mind the house! Who killed my— Who killed those people?"

"The Americans brought two Viet Cong to the village with their hands tied—"

"Americans? What Americans?"

"Soldiers. Three soldiers."

Only three. Not a full patrol, then. "And after that, what happened?"

Again that darting glance to the right and left. "The Viet Cong," he whispered. "I think they burned the house."

He was frightened almost to the point of incoherence. Lescaut saw that, despite his own torment, he would have to let the boy tell the story in his own way, however fragmented and repetitious.

Shortly after dark the night before, the boy said, the villagers had heard an explosion and seen a fiery glow mounting upward. Soon four people had come to the clearing—an older man and woman, and a young woman and a little girl. Two families had moved out of their huts to make way for the newcomers.

The villagers had been at breakfast the next morning when three American soldiers appeared, driving two Viet Cong ahead of them at bayonet point. Through the village chief, who spoke some English, they had demanded if any of the villagers had ever seen either of the Viet Cong. No one had.

"They believed us, I think, because they didn't shoot any of us. Just the Viet Cong."

Then one of the soldiers had seized Mai, and held her, struggling, while Lisa clung to her skirt and screamed. Another of the soldiers, waving an automatic rifle, had ordered everyone else into the jungle. All of them had hurried to obey except the two servants. They had protested. The boy, looking back over his shoulder as he scurried away through the trees, had seen the manservant actually seize the barrel of the rifle and try to force its muzzle downward.

"They got shot, I think. We heard firing."

46

"Where are the villagers now?"

"They are still hiding. They are afraid. I was afraid too, but when I heard you screaming, I wanted to see—"

"All right," Lescaut said. "All right." He released the thin shoulders. The boy scuttled away.

Why had they killed his baby, too? Because they were high on some violence-inducing drug, such as amphetamine? Because they feared that Lisa, young as she was, might be able to identify them? Or merely because she screamed at what they were doing to her mother, and they found the noise distracting?

And who were they?

Whoever they were, he would find them and kill them with his own hands.

He never found them. For two months he visited almost daily the United States Commandant's office and the United States Embassy. But although the Americans launched several investigations, the soldiers in every patrol in that area said that they had neither participated in such a crime nor heard of any soldiers who had. Furthermore, all the villagers, even the young boy Lescaut had questioned, now told a different story. American soldiers, it was true, had shot the Viet Cong for burning the house, but soon after that they had gone away. Then more Viet Cong had come and taken revenge by killing those people from the house.

One day more than a month after he had watched his wife's and his little girl's coffins lowered into the ground, Paul returned to the village in the company of an American colonel, a tall, quiet man who spoke Vietnamese. While Paul stood in silence, the colonel questioned one villager after another. It was Viet Cong, they said earnestly. Viet Cong who burned the house. Other Viet Cong who came and killed those four people.

Paul turned to the boy he had questioned that morning. "Then why did you tell me it was Americans?"

The reply came quickly. "I was afraid that there were Viet Cong listening."

They were all afraid. Afraid of the Viet Cong, of the South Vietnamese soldiers, of the American helicopters flying low over their villages. Afraid of anyone and anything that had the power to hurt them. And like most frightened people, they tried to please whatever powerful person they faced at the moment. Obviously both the Americans and the South Vietnamese officials would want to think that the Viet Cong did it, so that was the wise thing to say, whether or not it was true.

In the army jeep on the way back to Saigon, the colonel said, "It might very well have been the Viet Cong, you know."

"Yes." Lescaut did not think so. He thought that the boy's first, almost incoherent story had been the true one. But he would never know for sure.

"I'm sorry," the colonel burst out, "so damned sorry."

Lescaut nodded his thanks.

"But these things—" the colonel began, and then broke off.

Perhaps he had been about to say, "These things happen in a war." If so, it was well that he had thought better of it. Paul liked the man, but if he had said that, Paul would have smashed his fist into the colonel's jaw.

Three weeks later, despite his parents' pleading, he had left Saigon and gone to Paris. Two years after that his parents, still sorrowing over the little granddaughter they had idolized, faced with a seemingly endless war, and with their rubber plantation continually harassed by

48

Viet Cong, had also moved permanently to France. They now lived off the proceeds of the plantation's sale in a small town in southern France, where the climate was not too unlike that of the beautiful, tormented land they had left.

As for Paul, he preferred the gray and often drizzly city beside the Seine. He had grown older. His demeanor with clients—courteous, competent, and always rather formal—had become second nature to him. He no longer read the daily newspapers with bitter fury. The statements of the world's leaders, each praising the noble aims of his own government and deploring the wickedness of his government's adversaries, had become to him so much noise, like the incessant murmur of a TV set in a neighboring apartment.

When Millard—the first Millard—had come into his office that day shortly after his uncle's death, he had sensed within the first ten minutes what sort of proposition the man intended to make. Millard had talked around the proposition during two more visits before he finally had spelled it out.

Lescaut had been low in funds at the time. Delivering an envelope now and then during the course of his travels had seemed an easy way to make an extra twenty thousand francs—then about four thousand American dollars—each year. But the money had not been his main reason. He'd had a vague sense that he would be taking revenge, if only in a small and indirect way, for what had happened to his wife and child in that Vietnamese village.

As it had turned out, though, who would bear the brunt of his revenge? Not those three men, whoever they were, who had killed Mai and Lisa, but a young Ameri-

49

can Secret Service man, an elderly, not-too-bright woman, and a young woman who, from the look of her, also had a memory with which she found it hard to live.

Half of the Calvados was gone now. He started to refill his glass, and then checked himself. There was the drive to Geneva tomorrow, and the next day an even tougher one through the Apennines to Florence.

Chapter 6

The car moved smoothly along the highway that ran across the flat Lombardy plain. In her corner of the rear seat, Joan looked through the window. From her trip abroad eight years before she knew that more spectacular scenery lay to the south—Tuscany with its terraced hills, often topped by villages and ancient castles, and its handkerchief-sized fields where peasants followed plows, sometimes drawn by great white oxen like those ornamenting the terra cotta vases of Virgil's time. Here the fields were flat and broad, separated from each other by rows of wind-stirred poplars, and the men plowing the earth drove tractors. Still, she found the scenery pleasant, perhaps because she had slept soundly the night before in that Geneva hotel.

Her cousin, perhaps, had not. She was taking another catnap. Joan looked at her, huddled in the other corner with the collar of her gray fur coat turned up around her face. Plainly the men in the front seat knew she was sleeping, because when they exchanged an occasional remark it was in almost inaudible tones.

Feeling the driver's gaze, Joan turned her head. In the rear-view mirror his eyes met hers briefly. Then he looked straight before him.

That had happened several times, both today and during the drive from Paris to Geneva the day before. Each time she had felt a stir of something she had not identified as yet—curiosity, perhaps. Certainly he was a man to arouse curiosity. When they had stopped for lunch the day before, near the Swiss border, she had noticed the upper half of a new-looking paperback he carried in one pocket of his dark blue raincoat. Its title was, in French, *The Glory That Was Greece*. She had wondered about that. In a world flooded with paperback editions of best-selling fiction and nonfiction—books his clients might bring up in conversation—why had he bought Stobart's account of life in Athens twenty-five hundred years ago?

A strange man. She sensed that his was an iceberg personality, with only a small part of it revealed to the scrutiny of others. Was he married? She thought not. He had the indefinable aura of the loner.

With a slight sense of shock, she realized that this was the first time since that day in Central Park last November that she had speculated about whether some new male acquaintance was married.

The air was growing warmer as they moved south. Leaning forward, Lescaut adjusted the heater. He must stop looking at the girl. It was not like him to be unable to control such an impulse.

Perhaps part of the trouble was that he had found it difficult to get to sleep last night. Around ten o'clock, in his Geneva hotel room, he had received a phone call from the man he had first seen six days before in that Left Bank café. In guarded phrases, Millard had reminded him that he was no safer for having crossed a border. If he went to the authorities, he would still be extradited to a French jail.

Back there somewhere in the fast-moving Italian traffic—the trucks, the Fiats and Ferraris, the suicidally reckless men on Hondas—at least one other car was matching the sedate pace of his own. He was sure of it.

Because Muffy had wanted to stop for dinner at a wayside restaurant her friends the Harrises had recommended, they did not reach the red sandstone villa on its terraced hillside until well after dark. A guard in dark trousers, white shirt, and a visored cap opened the gate in the high stone wall. Joan noticed that the waist encircled by his gun belt had gone to fat. His salute as they drove past him, however, was delivered with military smartness.

The housekeeper, Signora Bellini, a blond woman with fluent although heavily accented English, had led Joan to an airy second-floor room. A smiling little maid with almost no English had helped Joan unpack, turned down the blankets and upper sheet on the four-poster bed, and then left her.

Joan moved out onto the terrace that ran around all four sides of the house. The air was soft, almost like that of late May in America's northeast, and scented by blossoming orange trees somewhere nearby. The blue-white radiance of a nearly full moon bathed the formal garden here at the rear of the house, revealing white statuary set among the dark, sentinel-like shapes of the cypress. Beyond the garden stood a long, low garage, built of the same dark red sandstone as the house. From its open door light spilled out to mingle with the moonlight.

The Mercedes stood on the graveled space in front of the garage. As she watched, Lescaut emerged and closed the garage door behind him. When he turned, apparently he caught sight of her there on the terrace. He hesitated a moment, and then walked through the garden and climbed the terrace staircase. Pulses quickening, she watched him walk toward her.

He said, "There is a Ferrari sports car in the garage. It is included in the rental of the villa. Perhaps you or Mr. Manchester might want to use it, and so I was making sure that the keys are in the instrument panel."

"Thank you. I hope it is well insured. From what I remember of traffic in Florence, it's hard to get through town without crumpling a fender."

"You need not worry. The car has proper insurance."

She realized that she need not have said that about crumpling a fender. A thank you, plus a pleasant smile, would have sufficed. By becoming chatty, she had extended a tacit invitation to linger.

He said in his somewhat stilted English, "Are you on holiday? I mean, do you have a position?" She could tell, from the forced tone of his voice, that he was not used to asking such questions of clients, or perhaps of anyone.

"Yes, I'm on the staff of a magazine. When my cousin invited me on this trip, I asked for a leave of absence." They were standing face to face. Because of the two-inch heels she wore, their eyes were almost on a level.

"Is it a sufficiently long leave of absence for you to remain with Madame for the entire trip?"

"Yes. I have a month. If she decides to stay over here longer, I imagine I could extend my leave."

After a moment he said, "I see."

Something odd in his voice. Chagrin? Annoyance that she would stay with Muffy until the trip was over? Surely not. And yet she sensed a tension in him, a conflict, as if he felt drawn to her, but at the same time wished she were not around.

He said, "I will leave the garage key with you." His blunt-fingered hand touched hers briefly as she took the key.

"You're not going to put the Mercedes in the garage?"

"No. I am not staying here. I have a place where I always stay when I am in Florence. Good night, Miss Creighton."

He retraced his steps to the Mercedes. After he had turned the car around on the graveled space, he eased it down the steep driveway to the street, nodding to the guard as he passed him. Well, that was that. He had hoped for some easy solution, hoped that the girl would remove herself from the picture in another week or two. It had been a slim hope, but the only one he had.

Joan watched the Mercedes' taillights disappear down the drive. Somehow the brief conversation with Lescaut had left her pleasantly restless, stimulated. Why not drive by herself into Florence?

She returned to her room and took a lightweight yellow cardigan from the drawer in which the maid had placed it. With the sweater around her shoulders she went down to the garage, unlocked it with the key Lescaut had given her, and slid the door back. The interior light came on automatically.

The two-seater was red and well-polished and not more than two years old. She slid behind the wheel. She was about to turn the key in the ignition when she heard footsteps crunch over the gravel.

Dan Manchester crossed the cement floor to stand beside her. "Hey! What's this?"

"They call it an automobile." She realized that she not only felt a little giddy, but sounded that way too. "It comes with the villa, Lescaut tells me."

"Fantastic. But why didn't he give me the keys? I'm supposed to be troop leader."

"Maybe because he saw me up on the terrace."

"Maybe. He's a strange one. A real expert with the

55

cold shoulder. Lukewarm one, anyway. But listen. You're not going to drive around in strange territory all by yourself, are you?"

"I'll be ten times safer than I am walking from the subway to my apartment after dark. Anyway, you're Cousin Muffy's bodyguard, not mine."

"That's true. In the case of your body, guarding isn't exactly what—" He broke off. "Am I going too fast for you?"

"Definitely." She smiled to take the sting out of her answer.

"And you don't want company?"

"Some other time. Not tonight."

"All right, all right. Just wait until I get you in a gondola in Venice." He stepped away from the car. "Back out. I'll close the garage door after you."

A few minutes later, completely unaware of a car that followed hers, she drove along a broad boulevard past apartment houses and luxurious villas set behind high walls. When she neared the Ponte Vecchio, that ancient bridge closed to all but foot traffic, she looked for a parking space. She found one, got out of the car, and walked toward the bridge.

The man following her made a quick decision. She would spend some time on the bridge. No newly arrived visitor ever hurried across that world-famous structure. And once she had crossed it, she probably would walk a hundred yards or so straight ahead to the next famous spot, the great square in front of the Palazzo Vecchio. The chances were excellent that he could pick up her trail there. If he failed to, he would just have to wait for some future opportunity.

He turned to his left and drove toward the nearest automobile bridge spanning the river.

Joan moved slowly up the Ponte Vecchio's slope between the shuttered stalls of goldsmiths and silversmiths, modern counterparts of the artisans who had offered their wares here since before Lorenzo the Magnificent ruled Florence. On the crown of the bridge, where the rows of stalls on either side gave way to paved areas, the usual early evening crowd had gathered. Some people looked at the lights of other bridges, their reflections like shimmering spears in the slow-moving river. Others stood with back to the balustrade, watching the strollers along the center of the bridge and the unlicensed peddlers who had spread their offerings—belts, ceramic ash trays, jewelry of some metal that resembled silver but almost certainly was not—on strips of felt laid out on the curb.

There were about a dozen peddlers, all of them young and long-haired, the boys in jeans, the girls in either jeans or ankle-length dresses. They were, Joan realized, part of the new international set, young people who drifted from London to Amsterdam to Rome to Florence, sometimes sleeping in the open, frequently going unwashed, and, if the need arose, turning mildly larcenous.

A girl in a blue granny dress, evidently a lookout, hurried up to them with a warning. Swiftly the peddlers rolled up their wares in the lengths of felt and thrust them into the backpack carried by a bearded member of the group. By the time two policemen, smart in their white-belted uniforms, arrived on the scene, the unlicensed merchants sat in a row on the balustrade, kicking their heels. The police, trying to look stern, issued a reprimand, and the malefactors made their straight-faced protestations of innocence. Within three minutes after the police departed, leaving the crowd's laughter in

57

their wake, the merchandise was again spread out on the curb. Four hundred years ago, Joan reflected, soldiers of the Medici must have waged the same sort of unresolved warfare on this bridge with itinerant peddlers.

She realized that she had enjoyed the incident. She also realized why she had been able to enjoy it. Something about the Frenchman had broken through the emotional numbness she had felt for months past.

Which meant, of course, that she was the same damned fool who had loved and trusted Brad Dillingham. If she again could feel interested in a man, why couldn't it be someone like Dan Manchester, who was not only young and handsome, but who would inherit considerable wealth someday? Why should she feel drawn to Lescaut, who was not young, not rich, and not even good-looking, at least not in the conventional sense? What was more, there was something strange about the Frenchman, something remote and cold and perhaps even dangerous.

Well, she need not worry. Obviously he intended to keep aloof from her. Within a month after she returned to New York, she would think of him with detached curiosity, if she thought of him at all. But in the meantime, she wanted to enjoy this sense of coming alive after all those dark months.

She would walk on across the bridge, she decided, and take a closer look at the Gothic bulk of the Palazzo Vecchio's tower, floodlit against the deep blue night sky.

Chapter 7

Standing at one of the long windows of her spacious bedroom in the villa, Muffy reached out and touched a wall switch. There, darkness was better. Now she could really see the moonlight, flooding the terraced front lawn and the boulevard, and glinting on the river beyond. The Arno, Mr. Lescaut had said it was.

Moonlight on a river. It reminded her of something she had seen long ago. Oh, yes, the cover on the sheet music for "Beautiful Ohio." There'd been a picture of a blond girl and a dark-haired man in a canoe on a river, with a great big moon up in the sky. Buzz had said the girl on the cover looked like her.

Not that they'd owned the sheet music. Theirs was a player piano, the first few years of their married life. On those few evenings when he wasn't at a meeting or out drumming up political support, he would sit down at the piano and pump the pedals. She would stand beside him, hand on his shoulder, and they would both sing:

"Drifting with the current down a moonlit stream
While above the heavens in their glory beam,
Beautiful Ohio, in dreams again I see
Visions of what used to be."

They'd sold the player in 1928 and bought an upright, so that Sara could start music lessons.

Thinking of that old song made her wish more than ever that Buzz was standing beside her now, his arm around her waist. Younger people would think that was silly, her feeling sentimental, even romantic because of the moonlight and an old song. But what did they know?

She wished that she and Buzz had gone to Europe by themselves, instead of on those junkets. But Buzz never felt he could spare the time to travel just for pleasure. He was always driving ahead, toward the next election, or toward membership on some more important committee. She had never understood what it was in him that would never let him relax for more than an hour or two at a time.

But then, there was so much that she'd never understood. She'd understood least of all those awful years in the White House. She'd always thought that if Buzz ever got there, he'd be happy. Instead there had been some of his old friends in Congress turning on him, and the newspapers turning on him too, and those young people gathering day after day opposite the White House.

She was sure that was what had hurt Buzz most, having the young people turn against him. Oh, she knew that a lot of young people had died in that war, that terrible war she used to think would never end, and that people a lot smarter than her couldn't make head nor tail of. All sorts of people had died in the war, including babies. Darling babies, with round faces and big dark eyes. But Buzz hadn't wanted those or any other babies to die. Buzz had loved children. When they were first married, he used to say, "We'll have four sons." It wasn't considered wrong to have big families in those days.

60

"We'll name them Matthew, Mark, Luke, and John, and maybe someday we'll see all four of them in the United States Senate."

They'd never had one son, let alone four. It was Buzz himself who'd finally got to the Senate, and from there to the very top. And the top had killed him. Oh, he'd lived for almost four years after they left Washington, but she knew it was the White House which had killed him. She'd watched it happening, day after day.

Well, no use brooding over the past. Think of being in this beautiful house, and of going on to Venice with Joaney and the Manchester boy. Joan was looking much better this past couple of days. Muffy had been really shocked when she met her at the airport in New York. It was because of that accountant, of course. How could Joan have thought that any good could come of an affair with a married man? Oh, maybe some girls were tough enough—cool enough, they would say—not to care whether the man was married or not. But Joaney wasn't one of them.

They'd thought they were so smart, Joan and the accountant, that day outside of Saks. Joan hadn't realized that she'd stopped in her tracks for a second at sight of him, or how strained her voice had sounded when she introduced him. Neither of them had fooled her, not for a minute.

This trip was the best thing that could have happened to Joan, especially with Dan along. She'd see now what a fool she'd been, and what a double fool she'd be to waste any more time brooding about that man in New York.

Well, she'd better stop mooning here at the window. Best to go to bed and read her book. She'd seen it in the window of an English-language bookshop near the hotel in Paris. It was *Lorna Doone*, a novel she hadn't read in years.

She switched on the lights and turned back into the room.

Chapter 8

For about twenty minutes Joan lingered in the big square in front of the Palazzo Vecchio. The great open space still swarmed with people. Some were taking flash photographs of Cellini's graceful Perseus holding the Medusa's severed head aloft, and of Michelangelo's David hurling his stone, nostrils flaring with proud defiance, white marble body awesomely beautiful against the palace's darker façade. She herself looked longest at the fountain, with its muscle-bound Neptune driving his wall-eyed steeds. One of Neptune's accompanying satyrs particularly fascinated her. His face, Magyar-eyed, hook-nosed, and slyly grinning, seemed to her the very image of cheerful rascality. She wondered what long-dead malefactor had posed for the statue. Perhaps some gypsy juggler who four hundred years ago entertained crowds in this very square, while an accomplice moved through the throng picking pockets.

Still in that mood of lighthearted venturesomeness, she walked over to the Straw Market. The stalls inside the ancient loggia had been closed for the night, but the bronze boar she remembered still stood there. His body was darkly tarnished, but his nose, rubbed for "good luck" by generations of the city's children and by visitors to Florence, gleamed in the light from a nearby street lamp. She too gave his nose a ritual rub.

63

What next?

To her amazement she found that, only three hours after that dinner outside Florence, she was hungry again. She looked at the entrance to a street which ran off the Straw Market's square. Eight years ago somewhere along that street there had been a *trattoria* which served excellent sandwiches.

She started down the street, past long stretches of buildings darkened for the night. Unchanged from the centuries when people traveled only by foot, horseback, or sedan chair, the street was both narrow and tortuous. The cobblestoned sidewalk, only about two feet wide, slanted toward the curb. Whenever she heard behind her the approach of a car or motor scooter, driven with Florentine recklessness, she moved closer to the buildings' front walls.

She turned one curve in the street, then another. No *trattoria*, spilling a warm glow into the night. Just these long stretches of darkened buildings, their stone faces illuminated by an occasional standard lamp. Was she on the wrong street?

Another car approaching, very slowly. She stepped off the curb and started across a narrow alley.

Something struck the back of her left leg. The car's bumper? She pitched forward, arms crooked at the elbows, hands instinctively spread, to break the impact of the alley's curb flying up to meet her.

Chapter 9

Carlotta opened the flat's front door for Lescaut, her round face smiling. As he followed her down the hall, she said over her shoulder, "I expected you earlier, maybe for dinner."

"The clients wanted to stop for dinner at Arnolfo's. And after I left them at the villa I had to take my car to a garage."

She led him into the kitchen. "Coffee?"

"Please."

He sat down at the table with its oilcloth cover of red-and-white checks. At the sink, she filled the espresso pot with water and spooned coffee into its basket.

He asked, "Giovanni not home yet?"

"No. At this new place he always works until eleven."

"How are the kids?"

"Fine. They're in bed now. Where did you have dinner, Paolo?" She knew that he never shared a table with his clients.

"I made out very well. Arnolfo asked me to have dinner in his private dining room." It was far from the first time that Lescaut, after a respectful withdrawal at the entrance to some three-star restaurant, had gone around to a side entrance, been welcomed heartily by some famous restaurateur, and invited to share food even more Lucullean than that served to the customers.

He watched her carry the espresso pot over to the stove. She was still a handsome woman in the dark, florid way of her southern Italian ancestors. But she was putting on weight. Since he had last seen her six months before, her hips had broadened considerably, so that now her outmoded plaid mini skirt displayed even more of her sturdy but well-turned legs.

Seven years before, when he had answered her newspaper advertisement offering a room, she had been a widow with a three-year-old son. For a time after that, whenever he was in Florence, he had shared her bed as well as her flat. Then five years ago she had written to him in Paris. She was getting married, but she hoped he would go on renting his room.

Their affair had been so matter-of-fact that he had no trouble in adjusting to his new status as just a part-time boarder and family friend. Occasionally Carlotta forgot and called him "caro," but not often, and never when her husband was around. If Giovanni suspected that Lescaut had been his wife's lover, he never gave any indication of it. Perhaps he kept in mind that he and Carlotta, especially now that they had their two little girls, needed the monthly sum Lescaut paid them to keep his room available to him.

"Who are your clients?" She lit the gas under the coffee.

He told her. Impressed, she asked, "What's she like?"

"The widow? Not what I expected. She's what the British call homely."

He had spoken the word in English. She repeated it. "Homely? What does that mean?"

"To the Americans it means unattractive. To the English it means homelike, or ordinary in a pleasant way."

"Like me."

He smiled. "Perhaps."

"And the FBI man?"

"Not FBI. Secret Service. He's all right. Too chatty for my taste."

"And the young woman?" Carlotta reversed the espresso pot. "Is she pretty?"

He said, after a moment, "Yes."

Leaving the coffee to drip through, she sat down at the table. She asked, chin resting on the heel of her hand, "Is that what's wrong with you, caro? This pretty girl. You like her, but she is rich, and will have nothing to do with you. That's why you sounded so strange when you phoned from Paris. That's why your face has that strained look now."

"You're wrong." His voice was almost harsh. "The girl isn't rich. She works for a living. Some sort of magazine job. And I'm not interested in her."

She studied him, obviously only half convinced. "It's time for you to be interested in *some* girl. You're getting old, Paolo. Almost forty. You want to be a bachelor all your life?"

He had never told her about Mai and Melissa. Except for his uncle, who already had known of their deaths, he had talked to no one about them since he had left Vietnam.

"What's wrong with being a bachelor?"

She shook her head sorrowfully. "Oh, Paolo, Paolo—"

The phone on the kitchen wall rang. His body tensed. Millard? During that phone conversation in Geneva, Millard had demanded this number.

Carlotta looked at him curiously before she shoved back her chair and went to answer the phone. She said,

"*Buona sera,*" and then, after a moment, turned to Lescaut. "For you."

He moved to the phone. It was his client, sounding upset. "Will you come back here right away, please, and drive me to the hospital? My cousin's been in an accident."

Chapter 10

A little before midnight Muffy and Dan Manchester emerged into the hospital corridor. Lescaut rose from the bench where he had been waiting, with the black beret crushed in his right hand. "How is she, madame?"

His client was smiling. "She's fine. In fact, she's mad as hops because the hospital says she must stay here overnight."

"Not even a shiner," Manchester said. "Just a bump on her forehead, and skinned hands and knees. Incidentally, she told me where she left the Ferrari, and gave me the keys to it. I'll drive it back to the villa."

Lescaut nodded, and then turned to his client. "May I see her for a moment, madame?"

From the corner of his eye he saw that Manchester's face had stiffened. Lescaut could not tell whether it was with surprise, or displeasure, or both. But the old lady said, "Why, I'm sure she'll think that's very nice of you."

He went through the louvered swinging door into the room. In a hospital nightgown, the girl was sitting up in bed, gauze taped to her forehead, bandaged hands resting palms up on the white coverlet. A metal-shaded lamp on the stand beside her showed him the leap of surprise in the great greenish eyes.

He said formally, "I hope you will not mind, Miss Creighton. I wanted to inquire how you are."

"I'm fine. The car was moving very slowly. Some drunk, I suppose, who lost control of the wheel for a moment. Some drivers who've been drinking drive like that, just as slowly as they can."

"The car drove on after it had struck you?"

She nodded. He noticed that the movement made the light ripple over her burnished dark red hair.

"Did you see the car?"

"No, I was too busy picking myself up off the sidewalk. Then a car with an English couple in it stopped, and they insisted upon bringing me to the hospital." She frowned. "It's absurd that I should have to stay here all night."

"Forgive me, but I disagree. These seemingly minor accidents can have serious aftereffects." He paused. "In fact, might it not be wise for you to be examined as soon as possible by your own doctor?"

"But how can I? He's in New York."

"I realize that."

When she spoke, after several seconds of silence, her voice was cold. "You're suggesting that I go to New York immediately."

"Under the circumstances, yes."

"You'd be pleased if I left, wouldn't you?" The driver of that car. Could he have been—No, he wouldn't have gone that far to try to make her get aboard a New York-bound plane. Why should he? And anyway, no matter what he was, she felt he was not the sort to strike someone down deliberately and then drive off.

His voice too was cold. "Of course I would not be pleased if you left."

"Oh, yes, you would. Why do you dislike me?"

"I do not dislike you."

She ignored the disclaimer. "Do I remind you of some-one else?"

After a moment he said, "No."

"I think that I must. Was it someone who once did you an injury?"

"No. As I said, you do not remind me of anyone."

Looking at the impassive face, she realized that she had indeed been a fool earlier that evening. She should have tried to ignore completely the physical attraction he held for her. From now on she would treat him strictly as her cousin's employee.

"Please leave," she said curtly. "I want to sleep."

Chapter 11

Before noon the next day she left the hospital and, with Muffy beside her, rode back to the villa in the Mercedes. Except when spoken to, Lescaut drove in silence. As if sensing that the Frenchman was in an unusually withdrawn mood, Dan Manchester faced toward the women most of the way. Without revealing the man's name, he told them in hilarious detail of how he once had been assigned to accompany a certain Cabinet officer and his kleptomaniac wife to Paris. The lady, eluding her husband's and Dan's vigilance, had slipped out of the hotel, and in two hours had stolen a tote bag full of merchandise—designer scarves, gloves, perfume, a gold cigarette lighter, and a nutmeg grater from a hardware store. Her husband and Dan, toiling in her wayward path the next day, had averted an embarrassing international incident only by means of profuse apologies and the payment of hush money here and there.

While Muffy was still laughing, Joan stole a look at Lescaut's reflection in the rear-view mirror. He must have heard Dan's story, but his face was utterly bleak, as if he had withdrawn into some harsh world where smiling was impossible.

Within three days Joan's bruise, which she concealed by brushing more strands of hair across her forehead, had begun to fade. In less than a week she was able to take the bandages off her hands and knees. By that time she and Dan were spending many of their waking hours solely in each other's company.

It was Muffy who had arranged that. Two days after Joan's accident, as the three of them lunched on the terrace overlooking the garden, she said, "Why don't you two take a drive in that little red car this afternoon? I'm sure you'd enjoy it a lot more than going to the Uffizi with Mr. Lescaut and me."

With amusement Joan noticed the glint in Muffy's eye, the determined glint of the matchmaker.

Dan said firmly, "Can't be done. Whenever you leave the villa, I go with you."

"Oh, fiddle-faddle. What could happen to me?"

"I don't know. But I know what could happen to me. I could lose my job."

Muffy dropped the argument. That afternoon both Joan and Dan accompanied her as Lescaut, at the Uffizi, led them from one lofty-ceilinged room to another. Joan and the Frenchman did not speak directly to each other, and when their eyes met, it was only briefly and by accident. She noticed that at first as he led them past ethereal Botticellis, brutally realistic Caravaggios, and sensuously tender Correggios, his comments had the mechanical quality of the professional guide's patter. When they reached the Raphaels, though, his tone changed, as if something beneath his crisply professional exterior could not help but respond to the paintings' serene beauty. And when they stood before Leonardo's "Adoration of the Magi," he fell silent for perhaps thirty seconds. Then he said, "Please observe how intensely human the foreground figures are," and went on looking at the kneeling, awestruck travelers from the East, the tenderly proud Virgin, the Child reaching out with an infant's curiosity to touch the gold vase proffered by one of the bearded Magi.

Muffy asked, "But what's all that at the top of the picture?"

Lescaut looked at the canvas's puzzling background, the ruined buildings, the mounted men engaged in wild combat. "Perhaps he was representing the downfall of pagan brutality. Leonardo's century was as bloody as any other, but perhaps, for all his genius, he was one of those naive souls who keep hoping—" He broke off. "No one knows with any certainty, madame, what the background means," he said, and led them to Verrocchio's "Baptism of Christ."

Joan looked back over her shoulder at the Leonardo. It was strange that Lescaut should be so moved by it. Perhaps it was because he, like the painting, was an enigma, one which she had no intention of trying to solve.

That night, toward the end of dinner in the villa's dining room, Muffy patted back a yawn. "Oh, dear. All those pictures really tired me out." Her plump face, in the light of the crystal chandelier above the oval dining table, was blandly innocent. "If you two will excuse me, I'm going to bed."

From the way Dan's lips twitched, Joan knew that he too recognized a matchmaker's ploy when he saw one. He said, "I was hoping to lick the two of you at three-handed bridge."

"Some other evening. Not getting enough sleep brings on my migraine. In fact, I think I'll take a migraine tablet before I go to bed. Now why don't you two take a drive someplace?"

They did take a drive, up the steeply winding road to Piazzale Michelangelo, parked at the broad square's edge, and looked down at the Arno Valley and the lights of Florence. The sight of the floodlighted Palazzo Vecchio's tower, visible even from that distance, reminded her of three nights before, when she had wandered with that new lightheartedness in the palace square, and then down that dark, narrow street.

One hand on her shoulder, Dan tried to draw her toward him. She resisted. He asked, "No?"

"No. I'm sorry."

He said lightly, "Am I so repulsive?"

"Of course not. I wouldn't even try to estimate how many women must have found you anything but repulsive."

"Not all that many. And anyway, it's right now that counts. Can't you at least tell me whether it's me in particular, or men in general?"

"Men in general, I guess."

"Can you tell me why?"

To her surprise, she found that she could. "I was very much in love with a married man. Then one day I found out he'd been lying to me. He had no real intention of divorcing his wife." She paused. "It's why I came on this trip. I hope Muffy doesn't know that, but I'm almost certain she does."

She felt his gaze studying her profile. "And because of that guy you mistrust men?"

"Yes. But it was my trust in my own judgment that was really smashed. I used to regard myself as a fairly bright girl." She added, in a lighter tone, "You think I should trust men?"

He pondered that, frowning, for a moment, and then said, "Damned if I know."

His frankness made her laugh.

He asked, "Want to drive down to the city and see

what the Florentines are up to at night?"

For a week after that, Muffy saw to it that they spent at least a few hours in each other's company every day. Twice at lunch she announced that she preferred an afternoon nap to more sightseeing. And almost every evening she retired to her room soon after dinner. Joan enjoyed the drives with Dan to the nearby hill towns—red-brown Siena with its steeply pitched streets, and many-towered San Gimiginano, and Fiesole with its crumbling Roman amphitheater. She enjoyed the evenings when they wandered on foot through the city's floodlighted squares. Several times that week he kissed her, expertly and not too demandingly, and she enjoyed that, too.

On the last night of their stay in Florence, Muffy announced that she would have dinner in her room. She was tired, she said, and wanted to rest up for the drive to Venice the next day. Free to dine out, Joan and Dan drove to a café on the river bank, a hundred feet or so upstream from the Ponte Vecchio. As they sat at a table near the glass wall overlooking the Arno, Dan began to tell anecdotes about that redoubtable man, Daniel Manchester, Senior, founder of Manchester Paint Products. How he had lobbied for a law banning the works of Thomas Paine from the public schools. How, until his employees had threatened to go on strike, he had demanded that they take their places on the production line fifteen minutes early each morning, so that on their own time they could pledge allegiance to the flag and sing "The Star-Spangled Banner." How he had kept badgering his senator to introduce a bill to revise the Declaration of Independence. "My old man felt that the phrase about all men being created equal might lead to

76

trouble. And so he felt it should read, 'equal in the sight of God.' "

Joan laughed. "Yes, I remember reading about that somewhere." After a moment she added, "But I can't recall reading anything about your mother, or ever seeing a picture of her."

He was silent for several seconds. "She didn't get around much. In fact, she was a semi-invalid for the last ten years of her life. She died while I was still in college."

"I'm sorry."

"So was I." His voice roughened. "I loved my mother very much."

She looked at him with surprise. Until then she had thought him a fairly typical Anglo-Saxon of his age and class—healthy, good at games, and caught fast in the male mystique that a real man never feels the impulse to cry. But now she was sure that when he had spoken of his mother's death, it had been through a throat that ached with unshed tears.

He saw her expression. "Hey! Did I do something right?"

She smiled at him. "Yes."

Chapter 12

Paul Lescaut was in his room, looking through a new guidebook to Italy, when Carlotta tapped on the door. "A call for you, Paolo."

His stomach knotted up. Millard? Almost certainly. He had been sure that the Russian would want to talk to him face to face before he took his client to Venice. "Thank you, Carlotta." He heard her footsteps go down the hall to the rear of the flat.

In the kitchen he picked up the dangling wall phone and said hello.

"May I speak to Etienne Giscard?"

By the book. Even when they were busy cutting each other's throats, these KGB types went by the book. "Speaking."

"Have you forgotten that we were to meet at the cinema tonight?"

There had been no such arrangement. How they loved their little games. Not for the first time it occurred to Lescaut that the Millards of the world—and the E. Howard Hunts and the Philbys—were men who had never quite grown up. Hence their choice of a profession which, with its passwords, its false names, its plots and counterplots, enabled them to act out fantasies which other men abandoned about the time they began to shave. Their games could result, though, in suffering and death which was very real.

"Tell me again where the theater is."

"Just the other side of the Ponte Vecchio. I'll meet you inside the theater in forty minutes. Sit toward the back."

There was a click. Lescaut replaced the phone. Forty minutes would give him plenty of time to walk.

He found the comparatively wide Via Calzaiuoli unusually crowded. Although according to the newspapers their "gigantic reunion" would not begin officially until the next day, the first contingents of veterans of the various Alpine Brigades had already arrived. They moved along the street in two's and three's and larger groups, some in business suits, others in knickerbockers and wool stockings that displayed calves thickened by skiing and rock-climbing. All of them, though, wore jauntily feathered hats with one side of the brim turned up. They ranged in age from a few grizzled World War I veterans to fresh-faced men who could not have ended their military service more than a year or so before. Lescaut saw the long-necked bottles of rough red mountain wine circulating among the groups. By tomorrow night some of them would be stretched out in doorways. Others would reach toward passing girls. A few, safe in the knowledge that friends had laid restraining hands upon them, would struggle wildly and shout threats of mayhem at each other. But on the whole, their roistering would be good-natured. Perhaps because they were less inhibited emotionally than most other peoples, Italians were less apt to turn violent at such mass gatherings as this one. Lescaut liked Italians.

Many of the groups he passed on the streets, and later on the Ponte Vecchio, were singing. The melodies were touched with sadness. The words concerned the beauty of their upland valleys, and the love of mountain girls.

If man was essentially a war-loving creature, as some people said, then why did the songs that soldiers sang, even in wartime, lack ferocity? He thought of how, during the Second World War the troops on both sides had sung, not the bellicose ditties written by home-front composers, but the wistful "Lili Marlene." Then he saw the lights of the cinema beyond the bridge, and lost awareness of everything except the coming interview.

He crossed the street and turned left toward the cinema entrance. A red Ferrari moved slowly along the street toward him. Manchester, at the wheel, was dividing his attention between the traffic and the upturned, smiling face of the girl beside him. Perhaps they had dined at the big restaurant on the river bank. Quickly, lest they see him, Lescaut hurried beneath the theater's marquee. Were they lovers by now, the tall young American and the girl with green-gray eyes? Probably. He felt a surge of envy of Manchester, and then cursed himself for a fool.

As he moved toward the box office, he glanced at a blownup still picture on the lobby wall. Beneath its Italian title, in smaller letters, was the English translation, *The Werewolf's Stepdaughter.* He knew what to expect: one of those cheap movies that some Italian companies were grinding out by the dozens—gory, kinky, and, in the American phrase, campy.

He bought a ticket and went inside. The few score customers were gathered in the middle of the house and toward the front. He sat down in the third row from the rear, leaving the aisle seat beside him vacant.

On the screen the lid of a black coffin stirred, then clattered to the stone floor of a cobweb-hung vault. A woman sat up in the coffin. Except for an eye mask covered with purple sequins, and an unconvincing cobra of some sort of plastic curled around her neck, she seemed to be naked. The cobra darted a forked tongue at the camera. Down near the front of the house, a youth gave a falsetto scream of mock terror.

Someone moved into the row behind Lescaut. He heard the creak of a lowered seat. Up on the screen, the woman was kissing the cobra. A few seconds later, Lescaut felt a tap on his shoulder.

"Don't look around," the heavily accented voice said in French. "Wait for about a minute. Then go down to the men's room."

Lescaut heard the man leave. He waited, then walked up the aisle, crossed a corridor, and descended steps. He found Millard standing at the mirror, tugging at a long gray hair which sprouted from his dark brown eyebrow. He plucked the hair, dropped it into the basin, and turned on the water. "That's right, comrade. It is not cultured to leave hairs in the wash basin," Lescaut thought, and then glanced toward the row of cubicles.

"It is all right," Millard said. "There is no one else here."

"What do you want?"

Millard turned to face him. "Information. You are taking your party to Venice tomorrow?"

"You know I am."

"You still have reservations at the Roncelli for your party, and at the Pension Guidi for yourself?"

"Yes."

"How long will you stay in Venice?"

"About a week. It depends upon my client." He paused. "Does it make a difference?"

Millard shrugged. "Not much. And after Venice you will go—where?"

"It depends upon my client. She has not yet decided."

"As I told you before, you are to decide for her. You are to convince her she should go to Vienna, with an overnight stop in Graz."

Lescaut was silent. It would not take much persuasion, perhaps none at all. Already his client had asked questions about Vienna—whether she could go to any sort of performance at the Opera House at this time of year, and what chances would she have of seeing those white dancing horses, and where could she listen to "scramble music—you know, with the accordions." Lescaut, who never corrected a client's mistakes unless it was absolutely necessary to do so, did not tell her that the word was *Schrammel.*

Millard took something from an inner coat pocket. "Here is the route you are to follow after you leave Venice."

Lescaut studied the map—a torn-out section of a European road map—which the other man had handed him. The route, marked lightly in red pencil, followed the highway north from Venice through the Dolomites and then on to the higher Alps. A few miles north of the little town of Weissdorf, the red penciled line turned sharply right.

"Probably you have never even noticed that road," the Russian said. "The entrance to it lies about a quarter of a mile beyond one of those wayside shrines and the ruins of a stone hut. It is an unpaved road and very rough and narrow, but it is passable. You will follow it for about ten miles."

Lescaut knew the road. He also knew that it ended near the site of a never-completed resort hotel, and near the small air strip upon which some ill-fated entrepreneur had hoped to see rich guests landing their private planes. Two years ago, before the project had been abandoned, Lescaut had inspected the site, traveling over that road in a construction boss's jeep.

He did not say so, though. Instead he asked, "And after that?"

"At the road's end, you will receive more instructions."

Lescaut kept his gaze on the map. The road's end. He was sure that it would be the end of the road in more ways than one. There his client would be seized and flown across the Hungarian border, probably to Budapest.

Lescaut long since had figured out why they wanted her. It could not be because of any information she might possess. For many years she had been living quietly in the American Middlewest. And now that he knew her, that guileless little creature, Lescaut found it impossible to imagine that her husband, either before or after his White House years, had ever confided any vital secrets to her.

And yet, properly handled, that little woman could become a powerful weapon in the hands of a Russian faction bent upon stopping the first tentative movements toward less hostility between their own country and hers.

And she would not be hard for men like Millard and his friends to brainwash. Already Lescaut had seen evidence of that. On the way from Paris to Geneva they had approached a crudely painted sign, perhaps as much as ten years old but still legible, on an underpass: "Yankees, get out of Vietnam." Looking into the rear-view mirror, he had seen confused sorrow in the old face.

He could imagine how they would keep telling her that her poor husband had been a victim of evil advisers. They might even present her with "evidence" that some of his Cabinet officers had urged upon him wholesale atrocities, such as using germ warfare. They would tell her that it was her duty to humanity to expose such men. They would tell her that in doing so she would not be a traitor to either her dead husband or her country, but faithful to the best in them both. And finally, tearfully, she would broadcast the speech written out for her.

And America, still divided, angry, and confusedly guilty over the war and its untidy aftermath, would react with fury. On both sides of the Iron Curtain, the hope of a less dangerous world might become just another failed dream. In America, those men who had always believed that the Devil was alive and well in Moscow, and that there neither could be nor should be peace until the Devil was utterly smashed, would regain enormous influence. So would their counterparts in Russia, those men who felt that the struggle against America must be carried on relentlessly and by any means, including the kidnaping of a gentle old woman.

Millard extended his hand. "It is a simple map. Surely you don't have to study it that hard to remember the route."

Lescaut handed the map back to him. "I think it is time you spelled it out. What are your plans for me after you take my client?"

"You will be hurt a little. A knock on the head, perhaps. Anyway, enough to carry conviction that all this happened against your will. And in time you will be suitably compensated. After all, it is to our interest not to lose your services."

Lescaut believed that even less than he had believed it in Paris. He said, his face expressionless, "What about the American Secret Service man?"

"We will take care of him. That need not concern you."

"And the girl?"

"She need not concern you either." He paused. "A pity that she did not go home after her accident."

"You can scarcely blame me for that."

"No." Millard's voice took on a jovial tone. "Perhaps you should have made an improper advance. That might have scared her away."

Lescaut felt a surge of anger. "Don't talk nonsense. She would have gone to my client, and I would have been replaced by another courier, and then where would you be?"

"It was only a small joke. What's the matter with you? Have you become emotional about that girl?"

Lescaut felt a sense of personal violation, as if the Russian had thrown a beefy arm around his shoulders. He waited until he was sure his voice would sound even, and then said, "I'm emotional about my own safety."

"Good. Stay that way." He turned back to the mirror, brushed his right eyebrow, and, with thumb and forefinger, seized another gray hair. "All right. You can go."

Unheeding now, Lescaut walked back through the crowds of singing Alpinists on the Ponte Vecchio. On the other side of the bridge, he was only vaguely aware that the Gothic tower of the Palazzo Vecchio now held blazing torches along its battlements and behind arrow slits, as it must have on fete nights for almost four hundred years. A plan, nebulous as yet, was taking shape in his mind.

He found the flat silent. In his room he stood motionless for a moment, and then walked to the closet and took down from its shelf a snub-nosed Mauser. He had bought it several summers before because his clients at that time, two nervous English widows touring Italy, had insisted that he carry a gun in the car.

He broke the Mauser open. It needed cleaning. He would attend to that in the morning, and then place the gun in its clip under the Mercedes' instrument panel. Right now he had something else to do.

He put the gun back on the shelf. Then he walked over to a table against one wall and from its drawer took a sheet of paper and a ball-point pen. He sat down and began to write.

Chapter 13

Standing at the front window of his dacha, Josef Brodsky watched his visitor alight from the rear seat of the long Zim limousine. It seemed to Brodsky that Vladimir Karpolovich moved with the clumsy deliberation of a large bear. Brodsky felt his strained nerves stretch even tighter. Already Karpolovich had kept him waiting for over an hour to learn of the final plans concerning the American widow. And at Josef Brodsky's age, anxiety was not good for a man. He moved into the short hall and opened the door before his guest could ring the bell.

The thin elderly man and the burly middle-aged one embraced. "Sorry I am late," Karpolovich said. "There are more cars and trucks on the roads these days. Soon we will have traffic jams just like the Americans, eh, comrade?"

"Yes," Brodsky said, and led his visitor into the small study. On the wall above the desk hung a large framed photograph of Lenin. Smaller photographs—of Brodsky's late wife, of their son in the uniform of a Red Army colonel, and of their three small granddaughters—stood on the desk itself, along with a tray bearing glasses and a carafe of vodka. Brodsky filled two glasses and handed one to his guest. Karpolovich, who liked foreign phrases, said, *"A votre santé."*

When they had downed their second drinks, Karpolovich said, "Well, Josef, I suppose you would like to know—"

"Not here. Let us walk on the beach."

Karpolovich looked at the older man with amusement. Often he had observed that men who had once served in the secret police under Beria seemed touched with paranoia. But still, to fear that his own country house had been wired with listening devices—

Then Karpolovich's amusement died. Brodsky had manifested no such fear during their last conversation in this house. And that meant that in the interval he had begun, as the English say, to get the wind up. "It is cold out," Karpolovich objected.

"It will be good for us. Exercise in the open is always good."

"Oh, very well."

From a chair back Brodsky picked up a tan woolen muffler, placed it over his head, and knotted it under his chin. "The wind affects my sinuses," he said.

It was odd, Karpolovich thought, how the human face seemed to lose gender as it aged. With that scarf tied babushka-fashion, Brodsky from the chin up might have passed for an elderly woman.

They left the house, walked past the limousine with its young chauffeur sitting stolidly behind the wheel, and went down a palmetto-bordered path to the beach. On this bright but chill afternoon no vacationing workers from Moscow or Rostov lay on the coarse sand, bodies reddening in the sun. Perhaps two miles offshore, an empty tanker bound for the oil port of Batum rode high in the choppy blue water.

When they had walked in silence for about a minute, Brodsky asked, "Well?"

"Calm yourself, Josef. We have plenty of time."

Brodsky wondered irritably why people said "calm yourself." Didn't they know that the phrase had anything but a calming effect?

Karpolovich went on, "You are not very familiar with classical history, are you?"

"No."

"A pity. This area of the Crimea is a most interesting corner of the world. Did you know that this was the legendary homeland of Medea? Did you know that the ancient tribes along this stretch of the Black Sea buried their female dead, but hung the corpses of men in trees?"

"No."

"In fact, those people differed so markedly from neighboring tribes that the Greek historian Herodotus believed that they were descended from remnants of an Egyptian army once defeated on these shores. Alexander the Great, however—"

His voice went on and on. Was he being deliberately sadistic? Or was he testing the state of Brodsky's nerves? Back at the dacha, he had seen the younger man eyeing him narrowly.

When Karpolovich finally stopped speaking, Brodsky said, "Very interesting, comrade. Perhaps you will loan me a book dealing with the Crimea's early history."

"I will be glad to." He paused. "And you will be glad to know that final arrangements have been made to bring the woman to Budapest."

Brodsky asked, more sharply than he had intended, "When will that be?"

"On the fifteenth or sixteenth, possibly the seventeenth. It depends."

"Upon what?"

"Upon the date the Frenchman starts driving her north from Venice."

"The Frenchman. Has it been decided what—"

"He will be killed. My reports are that he is unreliable. And he could identify two Soviet agents, including one —on our side. After this is all over, he will not be worth the trouble required to keep a close watch on him."

Brodsky said, dismayed, "He won't be killed right in front of—"

"Of course not. From the very first, we want the widow to be as well-disposed toward us as is possible under the circumstances. The Frenchman will still be alive when the plane takes off."

"And the American Secret Service man?"

"He will be left alive. As gently as possible, he will be put out of action, but left alive."

"Good," Brodsky said, and then burst out, "Still, I don't like it, our having only two men to do the job. Couldn't we use a larger plane, so that we could fly more than just those two into that valley?"

"Impossible. The landing field is a short one, suitable only for small, private planes. Furthermore it is in such a state, with the cement cracked in some places, that it is a tricky business for even a light plane to land and take off."

The older man said grudgingly, "Well, if that is the way it has to be. I gather," he added, "that the young woman you told me about last time has returned to America."

"Then you gather wrong. She is still with the widow."

After a moment Brodsky said in a strained voice. "Then you intend to fly both women—"

"Of course not. Of what use would she be to us? Besides, the plane will be overloaded as it is. With the addition of another hundred-odd pounds, it might crash into the mountainside after takeoff."

90

Despite the chill wind, Brodsky began to sweat. "What are you going to do about her?"

"Take her out of the picture."

"When?"

"In Venice."

Brodsky's voice rose. "Are you insane? If anything happens to the girl, the old lady won't leave Venice. She'll turn the city upside-down until she finds out what—"

"As far as the widow will know, her cousin will have returned to America. She will receive a telegram from the girl saying just that, a very apologetic telegram."

"But how can you induce the girl—"

"Comrade, I think your bad sinuses have affected your wits. The telegram will be telephoned in by someone else."

"What will the telegram say?"

"Must you worry about every little detail?"

"It's not knowing the details that makes me worry!"

"Very well. The telegram will say that she has received a telephone call from a man in New York, a man she was in love with, and that she is going to him immediately."

"But are you sure there is such a man in New York?"

"We are sure."

"How did you find out?"

Karpolovich struggled with a growing irritation. Why was the old man being so difficult? "One of our men who is shadowing the widow and her party telephoned a New York detective agency for more information about the girl. Someone from the agency interviewed the superintendent of the girl's apartment house. In America," he added jovially, "apartment house superintendents know everything that goes on. And over there the government doesn't even pay them to spy on the tenants!"

Brodsky did not seem amused. He said in a low voice, "But in reality, what will have happened to her? What do you plan to do?"

For a moment Karpolovich was silent. The girl would have to be disposed of. It would be far from the first time in Venice's long history that a well-weighted body was dropped late at night in the far reaches of the lagoon.

But best not to tell Brodsky that. He said, "She will be kept blindfolded and under sedation for a few days. Then she will be taken from Venice to the mainland at night, driven to a remote spot, and then released. By the time she is found, the widow will be in Budapest."

"I am glad she will be left alive," Brodsky said. "Not that I am turning squeamish," he added quickly. "It is just that we must think of how we will appear in the eyes of the world—"

"The eyes and ears of the world will be focused upon what the widow will be saying!"

He fell silent, relishing the thought of how, far more in sorrow than in anger, she would denounce the imperialists who had misled her husband. With even greater relish, he thought of the rage in America mounting like a great wave, with the hard-lining hawks riding back to power on its crest. There would be no more silly talk of detente, of relaxation, of tensions. Such talk had been only a screen, anyway, behind which the capitalists still plotted to destroy the Russian Revolution.

He laid his hand on the older man's thin shoulder. "So you see, comrade, there is nothing to worry about."

Brodsky waited until the hand was removed and then said, "I hate to contradict you, but we have not even touched upon what worries me most." He paused. "Do you still think the majority of the Politburo will stand with us, not with the Chairman?"

"When, as the Americans say, the crunch comes? Of course. Once the Americans denounce detente, once their cold warriors are again in charge of policy, what can the Politburo do but take a like attitude?

"Have faith, comrade," he went on. "We are far from being the only real Bolsheviks left. All along many Politburo members have distrusted the Chairman's talk about arms limitation." He made a contemptuous sound. "Arms limitation! Next thing you know, he will want to agree to on-site inspection of our missile silos. And that will be letting the fox into our Soviet henhouse for sure, won't it?"

Bending forward, he looked down at the old face framed by the muffler. The cold wind had brought tears to the eyes behind rimless glasses. "I am afraid this temperature is too much for your sinuses, Josef. Shall we turn back?"

Half an hour later, as the big car sped over a flat cement road bordered by palmetto-dotted sand, Karpolovich sat frowning in one corner of the back seat. He wished now that he had never brought Brodsky in on the plan. But he had known that Brodsky distrusted this drift toward a less wary, less hostile attitude toward America. And he had never dreamed that an old Bolshevik, trained in the hard school of Stalin and Beria, would turn soft.

But soft he was. And frightened.

How frightened? Enough so to go to the Chairman?

Karpolovich's hands turned cold at the thought of Brodsky, probably at the last moment, revealing everything to the Chairman. The first thing the Chairman would do, even before he called the American President on the hot line, would be to place Karpolovich and the few other Politburo members pledged to him under arrest.

No point, Karpolovich chided himself, in conjuring up improbable disasters. And no use to even toy with the idea of eliminating Brodsky, and not just because it would be dangerous, although of course it would be. Karpolovich and his still very small group would need Brodsky's vote in the Politburo. They would need all his prestige and influence as someone who, when a very young man, had been an actual associate of Lenin's.

No, he had best stop worrying. Brodsky's nerves, no matter how strained, would hold for the next ten days, which would be all that was necessary.

Just the same, Karpolovich was glad that he had misled the old man, not only about what was in store for the girl, but in two other respects also.

As the Americans said, it was always best to keep your hole card well hidden.

Chapter 14

At a steady fifty miles an hour, the Mercedes moved north toward Venice. With the Apennines behind them, they traveled through the fertile Po Valley, past dilapidated but picturesque farmhouses of pink or yellow or brown stucco, and broad fields filled with grapevines espaliered between mulberry trees. In her corner of the back seat, Joan tried to keep her attention divided between Muffy's chatter, and an occasional remark from Dan up in front, and the passing scenery. She could not. Instead she found herself unable to suppress a disturbing awareness of the man who sat behind the wheel. He had not spoken more than a few times since they set out, and then only in response to some question from Muffy or Dan.

In Venice, Joan realized, it would be harder for her to avoid the Frenchman. It would not be as it was in Florence where, thanks to the private guards at the villa, she and Dan had been free to roam where they pleased. Muffy would have no guards at the Venice hotel. Nor would she be likely, even as bent upon matchmaking as she was, to want to remain in her room for many of her waking hours. Being alone with a spacious villa and its gardens to roam through was one thing. Being alone in a hotel room was quite another. Muffy would want to go out in Venice with her courier-guide, and Dan would have to go with her. Unless Joan chose not to join them, she would be thrown in Lescaut's oddly unsettling company.

Because Muffy wanted to arrive in Venice by train, "like Katharine Hepburn in that old movie," they stopped at Mestre on the mainland. The two women and Manchester waited at the railroad station while Lescaut took the Mercedes to a garage. He returned in time to usher them into a first-class compartment, and then disappeared. As the train began its brief run across the causeway to the island city, Muffy said, "I wonder where he went."

"Probably out to the vestibule," Dan said.

"Why?"

"So he can get off the train the minute it stops, and grab some porters to handle our luggage."

"He's so efficient," Muffy said. "He thinks of everything. Why, he must have reserved this compartment before we left Florence."

"A man of parts," Dan agreed. "Art expert, linguist, chauffeur, and Lord knows what else."

Struck by something in his tone, Joan said, "You sound as if you don't like him."

Dan shrugged. "How could anybody like or dislike him? You can't get behind that formal exterior to the real man." He added, "If there is a real man. Maybe he's pretty much what he seems, a super-efficient automation whose only function is coddling well-heeled travelers."

You're wrong. Joan thought. There was a real man behind the aloof façade, a man both attractive and somehow frightening.

A few minutes later when they alighted at the cavernous Venice station, Lescaut was waiting on the platform. With him stood two porters with hand trucks.

They followed Lescaut and the two porters to the station's broad front steps. "Oh!" Muffy said, and stood stock-still, eyes taking in the broad Grand Canal, with barges and big rectangular waterbuses and water taxis and private motorboats moving over its wind-roughened surface. Joan looked with wry amusement at her relative's entranced face. No, Muffy would not be content to stay in her hotel room, not here. Joan recalled reading someone's observation that two sorts of people fall in love with Venice at first sight. Children—and those who remain children at heart—regard the island city with its network of canals, its footbridges, its maze of narrow streets where no wheels turn, as a kind of vast, rundown, but utterly delightful Disneyland. And the sad and world-worn find in still lovely but decaying Venice an echo of their own melancholy.

Lescaut had hailed a water taxi. It carried them and their luggage down the broad waterway, past tall houses with façades of white or blue or faded red. It seemed to Joan that the water lapped higher over marble front steps and against grilled entryways than it had even eight years before, when she had seen Venice for the first time.

The taxi stopped in front of one of Venice's finest hotels, its terrace decked with small tables and flowering trees in tubs. Before the driver had finished mooring his craft to one of the brightly striped poles, Lescaut stepped from the boat. He handed Muffy onto the landing platform, and then reached down for Joan. She had placed one foot on the platform when the wake of a speeding red fireboat made the smaller craft rock. Lescaut's other hand grasped her forearm and pulled her to safety.

A second later he released her. But that brief moment when he had held her, his face inches from hers, had made her whole body tingle. And she could tell, from the way his face had grown very still, that he had felt a similar reaction.

This was absurd. Here in Venice, too, she would have to find some way to avoid the man.

Lescaut followed them into the hotel, waited until they had registered, and then asked his client at what hour in the morning she would like to start seeing Venice.

"Let's make it early, say nine o'clock." Muffy's eyes were shining. "We'll ride in a gondola first, and then go to St. Mark's."

"Very well, madame."

As he turned toward the hotel doorway, his gaze barely brushed the girl's face. He went out to the terrace and turned right along the walkway that ran past a side canal. Through sunlight that had taken on the bronze tinge of late afternoon, he headed for Piazza San Marco and for one of the small hotels in the rabbit warren of streets behind the vast square.

When she had finished her unpacking, Joan walked down the wide hall and tapped on the door of her cousin's room. "Muffy?"

"Come in, dear."

As Joan entered, Muffy turned away from one of the long windows overlooking the Grand Canal. "I can't get over all those different kinds of boats. Why, I just saw an ambulance boat go by, with stretchers in it and everything." Then: "What is it, dear? Anything wrong?"

"No, but I was wondering if you'd mind if I went around Venice by myself for the next few days."

"Joanie! You and Dan haven't had a falling-out, have you?"

"Of course not. It's just that the article I have in mind

concerns what it's like for a woman to wander by herself around a foreign city. And before I write it, I'll have to wander, won't I?"

"Well, I suppose so. But I'll miss you. And Dan will be terribly disappointed."

"Oh, for heaven's sake! I'll be having dinner with the two of you every night, won't I? And sometimes after dinner we can go to the theater, or sit in the Piazza and listen to the band music." Muffy would not require a guide's service for either theatergoing or Piazza-sitting.

Muffy brightened. "So we can. And if I'm too tired, you and Dan can go out after dinner alone."

The three of them dined that night at a restaurant whose windows overlooked the Piazza. Midway of the meal Joan brought up the subject of her proposed article.

Dan said resignedly, "We'll miss you. But you're a working lady, and I approve of ladies who work."

Muffy asked, "Even after they are married?"

"Especially then. I speak personally, of course. My old man looks good for another twenty years, and government salaries aren't much. A working wife would suit me just fine."

He grinned at Joan. Had he, she wondered, been joking? Or had he just sent up a trial balloon? From the gratified look on her cousin's face, it was apparent that Muffy felt he had all but proposed.

Maybe he soon would. And maybe she should accept. With her disastrous taste in men, perhaps the sooner she was married to some fairly conventional male like Dan, the better.

"To get back to my article," she said lightly. "Any ideas about what I should call it?"

Dan said, "Since you'll be wandering around alone, and since Italian men are what they are— Well, why not call it, 'Pinched, but Not for Speeding'?"

"Joanie!" Muffy's face was distressed. "I hadn't thought of that. Perhaps you had better not—"

Joan laughed. "What you forget, Muffy, is that I am a veteran of New York City rush hours. Getting pinched is nothing compared to what can happen to you in a jam-packed subway car."

✤

Chapter 15

For nearly a week she spent most of her daylight hours alone. Aboard a waterbus, she rode past the many islands of the lagoon to the Lido, that barrier beach which, now the site of luxury hotels, has protected Venice for more than a thousand years against the often-stormy Adriatic. She visited the cemetery island of San Michele, with its legion of marble angels gleaming among the dark cypress, and its tribe of cats slinking among the tombs with the air of fugitive felons. On the island of Burano, inhabited chiefly by fishermen and their families, she walked down streets of ramshackle, brightly painted little houses, and in the public square bought a yard of lace from a girl who told her, in broken English, that for two hundred years the women of her family had made that sort of lace, and sold it at that very spot. And on Torcello, that all-but-deserted island which once was more populous than Venice, she visited what remained of a church built more than a thousand years ago, and for a moment had the illusion that she stood in some poignantly beautiful structure long sunk beneath the sea. The satiny surface of the gray marble columns had an undulating design, as if patterned by the wash of waves. Their ancient capitals might have been bleached and pounded by breakers, and there was a touch of seaweed green around each pillar's base.

Most of the time, though, she stayed in Venice itself, wandering across steeply pitched bridges and down narrow streets. Near the end of her second day in Venice she decided that she really might try an article on the joys of exploring a foreign city by one's self. She found it pleasant to stay for as long or as short a time as she chose in a church or museum. It was pleasant to sit at a table in the Piazza, with no conversation to distract her from her contemplation of San Marco's orientally splendid façade, or its four golden horses pawing the sunlit air.

She enjoyed, too, the brief but friendly contacts with strangers—chatty waitresses in the *trattorias* where she stopped for lunch, an elderly Yorkshire couple who paused beside her, as she leaned against a bridge's balustrade, and commented on the shocking fares the gondoliers demanded, and back-packers of both sexes who stopped her to ask for a match or a look at her guidebook.

True, there were also the Venetian males who followed her from time to time, at one side and a half-step behind her, murmuring what she assumed were compliments, or propositions, or both. But she found their pursuit more amusing and flattering than annoying. Besides, she soon discovered that she could rid herself of a pursuer by going into the nearest church—and Venice has almost innumerable churches—sitting down in a pew, and bowing her head. Such a display of piety, it seemed, was enough to quench the ardor of the most persistent follower. At least she always found, when she emerged from the church, that her admirer had vanished.

Each evening she joined Cousin Muffy and Dan Manchester for dinner, either at the hotel or some restaurant. They told her of their day's adventure—a trip to nearby Padua on the mainland, or a visit to the glass factory on the island of Murano—and she told them of her own.

After their first full day in Venice, Muffy reported that she had told Paul Lescaut about the necessary research for the magazine article. "All he said was, in that stiff way of his, that there are thieves in Venice, and he hopes you keep a tight hold on your handbag."

"I do." She paused and then added, almost against her will, "Did he seem offended? I mean, that I'm not availing myself of his services?"

"Offended? Why, I really couldn't tell, dear."

Dan said, "With that cold fish, who could?"

Late in the afternoon of their last day in Venice, a cool and windy but bright afternoon, Joan returned to the hotel. Because despite the wind it was such a beautiful day—the sky cloudless and the air crystalline—she sat down at a terrace table for one last look across the blue water of San Marco Basin to San Giorgio's rosy brick tower topped with a golden angel. A waiter approached, took her order for coffee, and then said. "There is a message for you, Miss Creighton. I will bring it with your coffee."

"A message? From whom?"

"I don't know. A messenger boy left it at the desk."

A few minutes later he returned with her coffee and a small white envelope. Wondering, she took out the note inside. In a neat, clear hand he had written:

My dear Miss Creighton,
    There is a matter of some importance which I must discuss with you. Will you do me the great favor of meeting me at seven-thirty in the small courtyard beside the church of San Stefano Martyr? You may reach it by leaving the waterbus at the Rialto Station. Walk along Calle Grazzia to the first

103

square, and then follow Calle Rudolfo to the church.

I shall detain you for only a few minutes. If you can oblige me in this matter, I will be deeply appreciative.

Yours sincerely,
Paul Lescaut.

Aware of quickened pulse beats, she read the note through twice. These past few days she had not caught even a glimpse of him. And now he wanted to see her alone. Why? And why had he suggested a church courtyard rather than a restaurant? Well, she could guess a possible answer to the second question. Perhaps he felt it was less presumptuous to ask to talk to her there, rather than across a restaurant table.

Should she ignore the note? If she did, tomorrow would prove to be an embarrassing day indeed. At eight they were to start the journey to Vienna, stopping overnight at Graz. It would be uncomfortable to ride for hour after hour staring at the rigid back of the man she had snubbed. Besides, his note said that what he had to discuss with her was important. She felt he was not the sort of man to use the word lightly.

Again she looked at the note. He had asked her to be there at seven-thirty. At that hour she was supposed to meet Muffy and Dan at the Quadri, the restaurant where they had dined their first night in Venice. Well, she could phone the Quadri, leave word that she would be a little late, and then take the waterbus to the Rialto stop.

She went on sitting there, undecided, aware that it might be unwise to meet him, and yet wanting to very much, and not out of mere curiosity, or to save him and herself from embarrassment on the day following. Then she stiffened with surprise. Paul Lescaut was coming up the broad steps to the terrace.

He saw her, hesitated, and then walked over to her table. "Good afternoon, Miss Creighton. Has Madame returned to the hotel?"

"Why—why, I don't think so. I thought she and Mr. Manchester were with you. I mean, my cousin told me that the three of you were going over to the mainland today, and then up the River Brenta."

"They went alone. I had to go to Mestre to check up on the car." He paused. "I came here to tell them that we cannot leave until nine tomorrow morning, because there is still some work to be done before the car is fit for Alpine driving."

He inclined his head slightly and started to turn away. She said, bewildered, "Wait! What about the note you sent me?"

He stood motionless and silent. Long since he had learned that when he did not know what to say, it was best to say nothing at all. She picked up a folded piece of paper from beside her coffee cup and held it out to him. "Here. Had you forgotten you wrote it?"

He read the note through, heart pounding, face immobile. Of course the girl had no way of knowing he had not sent it. She had never seen his handwriting. Nor did she know that the church of San Stefano Martyr had been closed for repairs for the last six months, its massive doors barred, and the gate to its cypress-shadowed little courtyard locked. But if she had gone there at seven-thirty, with the twilight deepening into night, he had no doubt that she would have found the gate open.

He handed the note back to her, relieved to see that his hand was not shaking. "Will you excuse me for a moment, Miss Creighton? I want to leave word at the desk about the later start tomorrow morning."

He went inside. At a desk in the lobby with its black marble floor and fluted gilt columns he wrote a brief note to his client. When he had handed it to the desk clerk, he walked to the broad front window and looked at the girl waiting out there on the terrace, profile turned to him, dark red hair lustrous in the late afternoon sunlight.

God! What could he say to her? Above all, how could he keep her safe until tomorrow morning? If his plan succeeded—the plan he had gone over night after night in his cramped hotel room—they would all be on their way to safety by this time tomorrow night. But how could he protect her until they left Venice?

Because for days now she had wandered alone and unharmed through the city, he had been lulled into a sense of security as far as Joan was concerned. They must have given up, he had decided, on their intention to get rid of the girl before they made his client, in Millard's phrase, their honored guest. Now he realized they had been waiting only for the eve of his client's departure. Did they plan to send a telegram in the girl's name, saying that for one reason or another she had left Venice? Probably. Probably, too, the telegram would urge his client to continue her trip. And the old lady, at least mildly upset, but still wanting to see the dancing white horses and hear the "scramble" music, would have complied.

He pictured what would have happened to the girl if she had gone to the churchyard through the fading light. A swift blow on the head. Then her unconscious body hidden beneath a marble bench or in some shrubbery until it was fully dark. After that, a boat ride to the deepest part of the lagoon.

Not for the first time, he felt an almost overwhelming

temptation to hunt up Manchester, tell him the whole situation, and leave it up to him to get the women safely out of Venice and eventually aboard a New York-bound jet. But such a course would not only bring a swift and deadly reprisal upon himself, it might bring immediate danger to the others. If Millard and his friends realized in time that they were about to be balked in their attempt to create one sort of international crisis, they might settle for another kind. He thought of gunfire, and his client's plump body crumpling to the railroad station platform, or to the walkway outside the American Embassy or the police station.

No, he would have to carry out his plan tomorrow. And in the meantime he would have to keep the girl safe.

Straightening his shoulders, he moved out onto the terrace. "I can only hope you will forgive me, Miss Creighton. It was very presumptuous of me to send that note."

Her eyes held an odd mixture of expression—puzzlement, curiosity, and something he could not identify. Self-consciousness, perhaps. "But why did you send it? What is the important matter you wanted to discuss?"

"It is important only to me, I am afraid. You see, I have felt that you have—avoided my company, particularly here in Venice."

Spots of color on the high cheekbones now. "Didn't my cousin tell you? I've been doing research for a magazine article."

"She told me. But—forgive me, Miss Creighton—I felt that perhaps that was only a subterfuge. I could tell that you were annoyed in Florence when I suggested that it might be wise for you to be examined by your own doctor. But I felt that perhaps I had given offense in some other way, too."

She looked down at her coffee cup. "No, you haven't offended me."

He said after a moment, "Then would you be offended if I asked you to have dinner with me?"

He was aware of sweat on his forehead. What could he do if she refused? Try to rent a room near hers for the night? They would know if he moved out of his hotel into this one that he was trying to protect her. Tomorrow they would be doubly vigilant, and that could wreck the plan he had gone over night after night, studying Alpine roads that were on the map, and two that were not.

She looked up at him, knowing that she should refuse, and said, "I would have to phone the Quadri. I was to meet my cousin and Mr. Manchester there in about an hour and a half."

He hoped that his face looked merely pleased, with no trace of the overwhelming relief he felt. "I know a very good restaurant on the Lido, and I have a friend who will loan me a motorboat. What is more, the lagoon is very beautiful around sunset."

She hesitated, and then said, "All right."

He glanced to his left. A waterbus was pulling up at the landing. Thank God is was a *rapido*, which made only express stops along the Grand Canal. He said swiftly, "It would be best to wear your heaviest coat, and perhaps a sweater under it. I will be back within forty minutes."

Fifteen minutes later he left the waterbus at the Accademia stop, moved swiftly along a maze of streets and over footbridges, and then down a narrow walkway beside a canal. He turned into a doorway. On one side of a narrow platform, motorboats rocked gently at their moorings in a twenty-foot-wide slip. Through a window in the wall on the platform's other side, he could see a plump, bald man bent over a desk.

Lescaut walked into the office. "Hello, Salvatore."

The man got up and stretched out his hand. "Paolo! I didn't know you were in Venice."

When they had shaken hands, Lescaut said, "Can I rent a motorboat?"

"At this hour?"

"My client wants to watch the sunset from the lagoon." He hesitated. "Will it be all right if I return the boat early tomorrow morning?"

"Ah! So it is a lady client." Salvatore sighed. *"Mama mia!* How I wish I had gone into the courier business."

"Could you put a couple of blankets in the boat's locker?"

"Mama mia!" Salvatore said again. "Is she pretty as well as rich?"

Paul answered, "Would you mind getting the blankets right now?"

"Sure, Paolo." He got up and crossed his office to a metal storage cabinet. "Mustn't keep a lady waiting, eh?"

A few minutes later, as Lescaut piloted the boat out of the slip into a narrow canal, he wondered if he should go to his hotel for the gun, the automatic which, tomorrow morning, he would place in its clip beneath the Mercedes' instrument panel. Swiftly he decided that he did not have time to do so. If the girl's hotel was not already under observation, it surely would be from around seven o'clock on. Someone would be watching to see if she took the waterbus headed toward the Rialto Bridge stop. And already it was almost six-thirty.

Chapter 16

Joan was waiting on the hotel terrace, in the same green wool coat she had worn when he first saw her at the Paris airport. As he moored the boat, she came quickly down the steps. He handed her into the boat and then, when she was seated, let go the line. He resisted the impulse to speculate about the man who sat reading a newspaper at a table near the one the girl had occupied. If they were being observed, there was nothing he could do about it except hope that no one would be able to follow them.

As the boat moved away from the landing stage, he asked, "Were you able to leave a message at the Quadri?"

"Yes." Her voice was stiff with self-consciousness. "I said I was having dinner with a—a friend I had run into."

He piloted the small boat westward down the channel between the main mass of Venice and the narrow island of La Giudecca. As they emerged from the sheltered channel onto the broad lagoon, the full force of the wind struck them. Joan took from her coat pocket a triangular scarf of green silk, put it over her hair, and knotted it under her chin. He asked, "Are you cold?"

"Not now. But I'm glad I took your advice about the sweater."

"It probably won't be this cold later on. The wind

often dies around sunset." He looked into the rear-view mirror. A barge, piled high with crates and barrels, had emerged from the channel. Behind it was a waterbus which, he knew, would soon head north toward the railway station. No other craft. Thank God, he thought, for the cold wind. On such an evening, there would be nothing but freighters and barges out here on the fifteen-mile stretch of wind-roughened water between Venice and the lagoon's southwest shore. If some small, pursuing craft did appear, he would be able to spot it immediately.

From the corner of his eyes he looked at the girl beside him. The tense way she sat with her hands clasped in her lap told him that she was uneasy, perhaps regretful already that she had come with him. How fragile she looked, how vulnerable to those enemies she was not even aware of, those men to whom she was just an obstacle to be gotten rid of.

Sky and water were so brilliant with sunset light now that he squinted against the glare. The girl said, "How far is this restaurant? When I crossed to the Lido on the waterbus, I had the impression it was only two or three miles from Venice."

"One end of it is. But it is a long island, and this seafood restaurant is toward the other end."

The girl said nothing, but he could sense her increasing unease. And in another few minutes, she would be even more apprehensive. He looked again into the rear-view mirror. No craft at all back there now. And ahead, only a freighter, perhaps loaded with Murano glass, making for the channel that connects the lagoon with the Adriatic.

Already he could see the island, ahead and to the right. Low and flat and thickly grown with grass, it was a deserted island, and so small that, as far as he knew, it had no name. A truck-farming family had lived there once, but apparently a fire had caused them to abandon the place. Nothing remained of the house except its foundation and a few charred beams. But a small shed some fifty feet from the ruins was still intact, or at least it had been three summers ago. Clients of his, two American couples, had picnicked on the island. A rain squall had swept in from the Adriatic, and he and the Americans had taken refuge in the shed until the deluge was over.

He changed course slightly. "Shall we stop at that island for a moment? The view of Venice from there is almost unbelievable."

After a moment she said, "All right."

Already the strong headwind was dying. He shut off the engine and let the boat glide gently to the rotting little dock. With relief he saw that at least from there the old shed still looked fairly sound. He stepped out, wound the line around a sharply slanted mooring pole, and then helped her across the dock and onto a narrow path, still not overwhelmed by the knee-high grass. She said, looking at the shed, "Do people live here?"

"Not now. Once there was a farmhouse, but it burned down. Would you like to stroll up there while I take a look at the engine?"

"What's wrong with the engine?"

"Perhaps nothing, but I don't like the sound of it, so I had better check."

She looked back at the shed. "Go on," he said. "There aren't any."

"Any what?"

"Snakes. Isn't that what you were thinking of?"

She laughed. "Yes."

"There are few snakes left on any of the islands in the

112

lagoon, and no poisonous ones, as far as I know. So go on up there, if you like, and then we will look at the view for a few minutes."

The girl moved away along the narrow path. Swiftly he crossed the dock, stepped into the boat, and opened the engine's housing. He took out the distributor head and dropped it into his coat pocket. He was back on dry land, looking toward Venice, when he heard the rustling sound of the girl's approach along the narrow aisle through the high grass. As she stopped beside him, he heard her draw in her breath. She said, "You were right. The view is unbelievable."

From that distance Venice, with its golden domes and rosy minarets, seemed to float between the sunset-flushed sky and the water that shimmered like shot silk. After a moment she said, "It's like a dream."

"Yes. Or at least the way dreams ought to be."

They went on watching, while the sunset colors faded from the sky, and the water turned from iridescent silk to gray satin, and the distant domes and towers became just a dark silhouette against the deepening blue of the horizon. He said, "Perhaps we had better go now."

When he had helped her into the boat, he got behind the wheel, switched on the ignition, stepped on the starter. There was no response. He switched the ignition off, waited for a few seconds, then switched it on again and stepped on the starter. Aware that the slender figure beside him had grown taut, he said, "Perhaps you had better get out, while I look at the engine."

She stood at the water's edge in the gathering dark and watched him open the engine's housing. He said, wretchedly aware of the false note in his voice, "Perhaps if I had a flashlight—" He opened the small locker just aft of the engine. As he had known he would, he saw

113

only the two blankets Salvatore had placed there.

He closed the locker, moved to the wheel, and again went through the pretense of trying to start the engine. Then he left the boat and crossed to where she stood. "I am sorry. It will not start."

Her voice was cold. "What did you do to the engine?"

"Do to it? Nothing, at least not intentionally. When I looked at it right after we stopped here, I tested the wiring to see if it was all right. It seemed to be."

Enough light was left to show him the cold hauteur of her face. "I don't believe you."

He said after a moment, "Will you at least believe this? I don't mean you any harm. I am sorry this happened. I am sorry I did not turn back to Venice as soon as I realized there might be something wrong with the engine. But you are perfectly safe here."

For a moment she was silent. Then she asked, "What's to be done?"

"If a boat passes close enough, we can hail it." No boat would pass that close. No boat would have any reason to be in this part of the lagoon at night. He had taken that into consideration when he had chosen this island.

She looked out over water that gleamed palely in the deepening dark. A few slowly moving lights marked craft on the lagoon, but they appeared to be at least two miles away. "And if no boat comes near us?"

"We will have to wait until morning. There will be fishermen out here then. Someone will take us back to Venice. Or perhaps I can fix the engine as soon as it is light. I can't now, with nothing but a cigarette lighter.

"I am sorry," he said again. "I imagine we will both be quite hungry before morning, but otherwise we will be all right. You will even be warm. When I was looking for the flashlight I saw that there are blankets in the locker. You can wrap them around you when you go to sleep up there in that shed. I will stay down here by the boat."

"In case another boat passes close by?"

"Yes, or in case a boat thief stops." Or someone far more dangerous than a boat thief. "I had best get those blankets so that we can sit down."

She did not answer. But when he had brought the blankets and spread them on the tall grass, she sat down, holding her back very straight, and curling her legs around her.

He said, after he had sat down a careful two feet away from her, "Are you afraid that your cousin and Mr. Manchester will worry about you?"

"Not really, not unless I'm still not there when they get up in the morning. Tonight they'll just think I'm staying out late with—with the friend I mentioned when I phoned the Quadri."

She realized now why she had not wanted to let them know she intended to have dinner with Paul Lescaut. She was ashamed of her own weakness, ashamed that she had been unable to resist a dinner invitation from a man who attracted her and yet gave her the sense that he lived deeply, and perhaps dangerously, alienated from other people.

He said, "I will get you back to the hotel by six in the morning. If I cannot fix the engine—well, there will be fishermen out here before sunrise."

Impulsively she turned to him. "I'm sorry I didn't believe you about the engine. It was unkind of me to think what I did, and worse to say it."

"No, it was quite natural." He felt ashamed. Well, if he were successful tomorrow, the lies he had told tonight would be more than justified.

For a while they sat, not speaking, in darkness relieved only by starlight, and by the light of a moon a little past its first quarter and already near its setting. The only sounds were the whisper of wind through the grass, the lapping of wavelets on the island's narrow beach, and, now and then, the plopping sound of another chunk of soil breaking loose to melt in the water. Hearing that sound, he was reminded that this little island, like the one which bore those splendid domes and towers they had seen bathed in sunset light, was being eaten away by the insatiable tides.

She broke the silence. "If I seem distrustful—well, it's really my own judgment of people I don't trust. Quite recently, I made an awful fool of myself over a man. In fact, that was the reason I took a leave of absence from my job and came on this trip."

So he had been right in thinking that she too had something she did not like to remember. "And do you feel better about yourself now?"

"Yes. At least I think about it much less." Abruptly she changed the subject. "Were you born in Paris?"

After a moment he said, "No, Vietnam. My parents had a rubber plantation there. They sold it some years ago and moved back to France."

Even though he could not see her expression, he was aware of her heightened interest. "Were you with the French army there?"

"No, I was still at the Sorbonne when the French finally gave up and left Vietnam."

"And you yourself didn't go back there?"

"Oh, yes. I went back after I had gotten my degree. I took over my father's office in Saigon."

She hesitated. Somehow he was sure what her next question would be. "Did you marry?"

"Yes." It was the first time in many years that he had answered yes to that question. "I was married to a Vietnamese girl. We had a small daughter. Her name was Melissa."

"Where are—"

"They are dead. They were both killed."

"Both—" She drew in her breath. "Oh, I'm so terribly sorry. Forgive me for asking. I know you don't want to talk about it."

"But I do." He did. He did not know why. Perhaps it was because he knew that he and the girl beside him might be dead by this time tomorrow night. Senselessly dead, like Mai and Lisa, victims of forces unleashed by powerful, distant men.

"If you think you can listen," he said, "I would like to tell you."

She turned her head and looked out over the dark water. "I can listen."

"It was in nineteen sixty-five. Because of the Viet Cong, Saigon had become a dangerous city. I was afraid for my wife and our little girl. I took them to a country house owned by relatives of my wife. I thought they would be safe there."

He went on, telling of the burned plantation house, and the nearby village empty except for the two dead Viet Cong, and the two dead servants, and his dead wife and little girl. He spoke of the frightened boy he had questioned, and then of the long, maddening months when he had tried to find the murderers of his wife and child, and then of the circle of villagers, all smiling the fixed smiles of the terrified, and saying yes, yes, it was Viet Cong who did it.

"I went to Paris, finally, and joined my uncle in the courier business, and never went back to Vietnam."

The girl had been crying quietly, her cheek pillowed on her updrawn knees. She said in a muffled voice, "How you must hate Americans."

"No. Maybe I once did, but not now."

"But if it was—"

"It might have been Viet Cong. It could very well have been."

"But you think it was Americans."

"I think it was soldiers who did it," he said wearily. "It is the sort of thing that French soldiers could have done, or Chinese, or Spaniards, or any other kind you could mention. In every army there are a few men like that. A war gives them a chance to do almost anything they please to helpless people, and they use that chance."

She sat up and groped in her shoulder bag for a handkerchief. She wiped her eyes, blew her nose. "When you came to that hospital in Florence," she said, "I asked you if I reminded you of someone. You said no. But I do remind you of someone, don't I?"

"Yes. Her hair was dark, of course, and she was much shorter than you. But she had that fine-boned look, and beautiful legs."

Silence. He knew that if he reached out for her, she would come into his arms. She thought she knew all about him now—the reason for his withdrawn manner, even the reason for his attempt in Florence to persuade her to return to New York.

But she did not know all about him. She did not know that in his cynicism, his cold disgust with the human race, he had sold himself to the first Millard, and thereby delivered himself into the hands of the second Millard.

And he could not tell her about it, not yet. The success of his plan to save her, and her two companions and himself, depended upon his not telling them until they were well on their way to safety. And once she knew the truth about him, she might forever after loathe herself for waiting, as he could tell she was waiting now, for him to reach out for her.

He said, "Do you think you can sleep now? I'll carry the blankets up to the shed."

When she spoke, her voice was stiff. "I'm warmly dressed. You keep one blanket."

"Very well."

By starlight, they walked up the narrow path to the shed. He flicked on his cigarette lighter and surveyed the earthen floor, strewn with wisps of moldy straw. "It is certainly not the Ritz," he said, and handed her the folded blanket.

She smiled the bright, proud smile of the rejected. "It will do."

He looked at the lovely face, and found himself unable to resist reaching out to touch her cheek. "Good night," he said, and released his thumb from the cigarette lighter.

He walked back to the shore and, on the crushed grass where he and the girl had sat, rolled himself up in the other blanket, knowing that the first light would wake him.

Chapter 17

With an exclamation of disgust, the man with the bushy eyebrows replaced the phone in its cradle. Across the room, a woman called Sofia looked up from her knitting. "Lescaut still doesn't answer?"

"No." He got up, moved to a window, and stared across an alley only four feet wide at the shuttered window of the moldering house opposite. Damn Venice, with its rat maze of streets and side canals that made it hard to keep track of anyone, even under the best of circumstances. And damn Hentzel for drinking the water here, after he'd been warned to use nothing but mineral water.

Hentzel had been supposed to watch that hotel tonight, and follow the girl when she left it. Instead, he was where he had been all day—in a back room of this flat, staggering weak and green-faced from his bed to the bathroom and then back again. Because he felt he could spare neither of the two men who were to wait for the girl in the courtyard beside the church, Millard had been forced to let the hotel remain unwatched.

Where was the girl now? He had no idea. He only knew that she had failed to show up in the courtyard. And all the clerk at her hotel could tell him was that Miss Creighton had left her key at the desk, shortly before seven o'clock, and gone out.

Maybe she had intended to go to the courtyard. Certainly when he had dispatched the note he had been sure she would take the bait. Feminine curiosity alone might have been motive enough. But he had counted on something else, something he had seen in her face one day in Florence at the Uffizi. As he moved past a doorway, he had thrown a quick look inside. Flanked by the old lady and the Secret Service man, Lescaut had been directing their attention at a picture. The girl, though, had not been looking at the canvas. she had been looking at the Frenchman, her face a study in unwilling fascination.

The very fact that she had stayed out of Lescaut's company, both in Florence and here in Venice, had seemed to Millard proof of how strongly she was drawn to the courier. She was ashamed and disturbed—as what bourgeois American girl would not be—by her feeling for the hard-bitten Frenchman with the broken nose and the cold gray eyes. And so she had avoided him. But Millard had been sure she could not resist the direct invitation of that note.

Perhaps she had not resisted. Perhaps she had met with a serious accident on her way to the courtyard, and right now lay in some hospital. In that case, all the careful planning for tomorrow would prove to have been wasted effort. The old lady would not start north. She would stay here until the girl was able to travel, and then, in all probability, take her back to New York.

But no matter where the girl was now, he himself had failed—and been left completely in the dark—all because one man had been too careless, or too miserly, to buy himself mineral water.

The click of those knitting needles irritated him. He turned around. "Do you have to do that?"

"Why shouldn't I?" She was a blond woman of about

thirty-five, not fat, just heavy-boned. Although she was only half Russian—her mother had been born in Naples—her broad face was completely Slavic. "It's better than walking the floor, the way you have been doing."

He looked at her with a near-hatred he knew was unreasonable. Sofia, unlike Hentzel, was a good operative. Ten days ago she had asked for a maid's job at the hotel where Lescaut's party was to stay, and, with the peak tourist season coming on, had been promptly hired. Within two days after she had gone to work she had obtained an extra passkey, one she did not have to turn in at the end of her shift. Yes, she had been prepared to do her part tonight. It was not her fault that everything had gone wrong.

He walked back to a sagging-springed armchair of dark red plush, sat down, and reached for the phone on the plastic-topped table beside it. A moment later, in English, he spoke to a desk clerk. No, Mr. Lescaut had not returned.

He hung up. Could Lescaut and the girl be together somewhere? No, there was almost no chance of that. During a phone conversation the previous night Lescaut had mentioned that he was going to Mestre today to make sure the garage there had checked his car over thoroughly. Millard himself had seen Lescaut board the train early in the afternoon. Probably he'd had dinner in Mestre. And even if he had returned to Venice before seven, Millard could think of no reason why the Frenchman should have gone to his client's hotel and perhaps encountered the girl there. Certainly all these days in Venice he had avoided that luxurious establishment at the lower end of the Grand Canal. Usually when the old lady had wanted his services as a guide to some museum or church, Lescaut had met her and her escort there.

Perhaps his client had preferred it that way. Or perhaps Lescaut himself had suggested the arrangement. After all, he could not help but be aware that the girl was avoiding him.

A thought that had turned Millard's palms sweaty several times tonight again assailed him. Had Lescaut gotten in touch with the police or the French or American consul? No, Millard assured himself again, if Lescaut had intended to turn informer, he would have done so many days ago. It was apparent by now that the Frenchman, like almost everyone else, valued his own skin above all. He would go along with his instructions tomorrow, desperately trying to believe in the promise that he would be left alive.

A piece of paper lay beside the phone. On it Millard had written the telegram which, if all had gone well, Sofia would have phoned in to the telegraph office more than an hour ago. He picked up the paper. The wire was to have been addressed to the widow. Its text read:

> The man I want very much to marry has telephoned me from New York. He will soon be free and wants me to come to him right away. I am taking the train to Milan, and will fly from there to New York. Because I know how much you will disapprove, I am ashamed to face you. Please have a good time in Vienna. And please try to forgive me. Love, Joan.

Again he looked at Sofia, thinking of how, by now, her work and his in Venice should have been over. By now the girl's well-weighted body should have slipped into the lagoon. Sofia should have phoned in the telegram, and then gone immediately to the hotel, used her passkey to enter the girl's room, and hidden her luggage tempo-

123

rarily behind a tall stack of linen in a storage closet.

Well, he had failed. If he'd had more operatives— But his superiors in Moscow had sent word that he was to get along with what he had. Easy enough for them to say.

The phone beside him rang. Miserably aware of who the caller must be, he lifted the instrument.

A voice said in Russian, "Did the interview with the young lady go all right?"

"No, she did not appear." Millard had to force the words out. "I have no idea why, and no idea where she is now."

Silence. But Millard could feel the other man's anger and alarm throbbing over the line. Millard said, "I am afraid the interview will have to take place tomorrow, after the other lady's departure."

Again silence. Then: "If that's the way it has to be." He hung up, none too gently.

Millard replaced the phone. Well, that was that. The girl would be killed tomorrow there in the valley, after the plane took off with the widow aboard. As for Millard himself, all he had to do tomorrow was to follow the Mercedes north along the highway until it reached that almost impassable side road. After that he would still follow, but keep well out of sight, lest the Mercedes' passengers suspect that they were being driven into a trap.

He looked at the phone. Call Lescaut again? No, why bother? The Frenchman, instead of getting the sleep he needed, must be in some café trying to get so drunk that he wouldn't think about tomorrow.

But that was no reason why he himself should not try to sleep. He stood up. "I'm going to bed."

Sofia looked up, nodded, and returned her gaze to the flashing needles.

124

Chapter 18

The first light awoke him. He unrolled himself from the blanket and, feeling a little stiff after his night on the ground, moved across the small dock to the boat. He restored the distributor head, and then went forward to the wheel. He switched on the ignition, stepped on the starter. The engine responded with a roar.

When he had switched off the engine, he got out of the boat and stood for a moment in the tall grass, looking out over the lagoon. On this windless morning it was like a vast sheet of gray glass. Already the water was dotted with chunky, high-prowed fishing boats, some moving slowly, others motionless. Those nearby cast mirror images on the smooth water. He turned and moved up the narrow path.

The engine's roar had awakened Joan. She now sat curled up on the blanket on the shed's dirt floor, one hand holding an opened powder compact, the other running a comb through her hair.

She no longer felt hurt and puzzled by his failure to take her in his arms the night before. Soon after he left her she had realized what must be the reason. Not indifference to her. Every instinct told her that he found her far more than just desirable. But a man numbed by the brutal murder of a beloved wife and child could not help but fear a reawakening of his ability to love. She was sure that the only women he'd had all these years were ones for whom he could feel, at most, a casual liking and good will.

Could there be any future for the two of them? She did not know. She only knew that just the faint sound of his approach through the tall grass was enough to set her heart racing.

He stopped in the shed's doorway. "So you are awake."

She smiled at him. "And you got the boat started."

He nodded. "A loose wire. I missed it last night, but this morning it took me only a second to fix it. We had better go," he added. "With any luck at all, I should be able to get you back to the hotel while everyone but the night staff is still asleep."

She put comb and compact in her shoulder bag, and then took the hand he extended to her. Brushing wisps of straw from the sleeves and skirt of her coat, she followed him down the path.

At full throttle, they moved out onto the lagoon. Now sky and water were streaked with rose and gold. Venice, which only minutes before had been a dark smudge on the horizon, again seemed to float, domed and minareted, like some magical city out of an Arabian fairy tale. Lescaut reflected that at this distance, where one could not see the scabrous plaster of the ancient houses or once-splendid marble entry steps now glimmering below green canal water, it was almost impossible to believe that the city was a thousand years old. It looked as newly created as the morning.

He said, "How did you sleep?"

"Quite well, once I got to sleep. Did you get any sleep?"

"Enough." At least he hoped it was enough. But then,

it might turn out that no amount of sleep would have made any difference. He began to think of all that could go wrong. That narrow road. If there was no longer a way of turning off it— Abruptly he suppressed the thought. When the time came, he would just have to do his best, and hope that it was good enough.

They entered the Giudecca channel. "Hungry?" he asked.

"Ravenous."

"Then get a good breakfast. It may be a long time before lunch." As for dinner, it might be that none of the four of them would have dinner ever again.

He could see the hotel landing stage now. "Do you think that the three of you can get to the railroad station by yourselves?" He had other things to do. He had not even packed his duffel bag for the trip north, let alone gone over for one last time that map he had drawn. And he had to make that call to Carlotta in Florence.

"I'm sure we can."

No one was on the landing stage or the hotel terrace. No one as yet had even unstacked the chairs from the tables under the bright yellow awning. He moored the boat, stepped onto the landing, and extended his hand. When she stood beside him, he said, "Then I shall see you at the railroad station at nine."

"Yes."

"Joan."

Faint color appeared in her face. It was the first time he had called her that. "Yes?"

He hesitated, and then said swiftly, "I am sorry." Sorry that he had not called the police that day ten years before when the Russian agent first came into his office. Sorry that she was involved in something that might mean her death. Sorry that he had not been able to think of a surer way of saving all of them.

She said, "About the boat, you mean? You couldn't help that." She herself was very glad that the boat's engine had failed. She smiled at him. "See you at nine."

He watched her until she disappeared inside the hotel. Then he got into the motorboat and piloted it along the Grand Canal and then a narrow side canal to the boat rental slip.

He was in his hotel room half an hour later when the phone rang. He picked it up.

Millard must have been in a sour humor indeed, because this time he did not bother with his little formula. "Where the hell were you last night? I kept calling until almost eleven."

"That's none of your business."

"I hope you weren't getting drunk," Millard said coldly. "You'll need to keep your wits about you today."

"I wasn't drinking."

"Then what were you doing?"

"I told you. I'm here now. Where I was last night is none of your business."

After a moment Millard gave a short laugh. "A personal friend, or a professional lady?" When Lescaut did not answer, Millard went on, "Were you afraid it was your last night on earth? It won't have been, if you watch your step today."

"Why have you called me?"

"To make sure when you are meeting the two women and the man at the railroad station. Is it still eight o'-clock?"

"No, nine. The garage in Mestre won't have the car ready until nine-thirty." He waited for a moment, hoping his voice would hold the right note of surprise. "Did you say two women? The girl will be there too? I'd

128

gathered that you intended—"

"Never mind what you gathered," Millard snapped. "Just watch yourself all the way, because that's what we'll be doing. And above all," he went on, "watch yourself at the Austrian border. If there is any sign that you are talking to the border guards any longer than necessary, we will open fire on your car right then and there, and never mind that in turn the border guards may kill one or all of us."

When Lescaut did not reply, Millard added, "I know it is hard for someone like you to understand, but to us some things are more important than our own skins."

Chapter 19

Lifting one hand from the wheel, Lescaut adjusted the sunshade on his side of the car. Midafternoon sunlight, reflected off a white peak a few miles ahead down the highway, was striking into his eyes. Even though these Alpine valleys were dotted with spring flowers, snow still blanketed the high mountains.

He looked into the rear-view mirror. The black Volvo, with two men in the front seat and one in the rear, was still there, of course. It had been there, never more than three cars behind, ever since they had started north from the mainland opposite Venice. It had followed them into the Dolomites, with their pretty little villages and their isolated peaks which eons of wind and rain and snow had carved into fantastic shapes—giant chimneys and towers and crusaders' castles. At the Austrian border, the Volvo had been right behind them at the barrier, so close that he could see a shaving cut on the chin of the thick-set, red-haired man who sat at the wheel, and the cold warning in the eyes of Millard, sitting there beside the driver. When Lescaut and his party had stopped at an inn for lunch, the Volvo had waited, parked about a hundred yards back along the highway. And now here in the higher Alps, with their jagged peaks rising wave upon wave, the Volvo was still back there, at the moment passing a blue tourist bus.

Beside him, Manchester leaned forward, looked through the windshield at the jagged peaks ahead, and said, "Wow!" At the outset of today's journey he had been his usual voluble self. Even as they moved through the Dolomites' fantastic scenery, he had kept up a steady stream of talk about the traffic, and the condition of the road, and sports, particularly his own football career as a defensive end at Yale. But here in the high Alps, as if awed by the almost threatening majesty of peaks which loomed above drifting clouds, he had been much quieter.

Joan had said little at any time since they had set out that morning. Now Lescaut's eyes met hers in the rearview mirror. As always when that had happened today, she gave him a grave smile. And as always, he felt a bittersweet longing for what there was almost no chance they would ever have together. It was strange, after all these years of self-imposed detachment from others, to feel such an emotion. It was painful, too, like a knife cutting through scar tissue to an old wound.

He turned a curve, and then his heart began to pound. Ahead was the wayside shrine, with its crucified Christ beneath a shallow peaked roof. Beyond that was the ruins of a stone hut. And beyond that, he knew, a hundred feet or so past the next curve, was the entrance to the side road he must take. The Volvo had moved close up behind him now, to make sure he turned off the highway.

He did. The dirt side road, carved out of the mountainside above a U-shaped valley, was rough, tortuous, and, he knew, so narrow that there was no room for vehicles to pass each other. On the left-hand side, the boulder-strewn earth dropped sharply away to the valley floor.

Manchester's face swiveled toward him. "Hey! What gives? Why are we turning off?"

131

"Detour," Lescaut said briefly. After a moment he added, "We'd have run into several miles of highway construction if we had kept on the main road. This way we will get around it."

He glanced into the mirror. No sign of the Volvo yet. But he knew it was back there, waiting until he'd had time to turn the first curve in this narrow dirt road before it began to follow him.

He turned the curve. Beside him Manchester said, "Well, I guess you know what you're doing, but this sure doesn't look like much of a road to me."

"It is passable." Lescaut was sure it was. Otherwise he would not have been ordered to take it. The question, he thought, feeling his stomach tighten into a cold knot, was whether the Mercedes could get over that other road, nothing more than a cart track, which joined this one about a half mile before its end.

He drove on down the winding road, grateful that the two women as well as Manchester were silent. Occasionally he glanced into the mirror to reassure himself that the Volvo was still lying well back and out of sight.

He turned a curve. About a hundred yards ahead the road curved again, around a treeless granite bluff that rose as sheerly as the prow of a gigantic battleship. Between him and that bluff lay the entrance to a narrow declivity in the mountainside, and the track running along it.

He drove very slowly now, eyes scanning the right-hand side of the road. There just ahead was the track's entrance, screened by tall mountain ferns now, so that if he had not known it was there he would never have noticed it.

He turned onto the cart track. No sunlight here, with the pines touching overhead. On his left a stream rushed

132

down toward the spillway which funneled it under the dirt road they had just left, and then down into the U-shaped valley.

"What the hell!" Manchester exclaimed.

"Didn't you see the sign back there a minute ago? It said, 'Danger. Rock slide ahead.'"

"I didn't see any sign. And anyway, why didn't you try to turn around?"

"On that narrow road? Probably we would have been at the bottom of the valley by now."

Looking grim, Manchester slumped lower in the seat. "Well, I hope you know what you're doing."

Lescaut hoped so too. He had never tried to drive along this narrow track. That construction boss, though, had said that some of his workers, bunking temporarily in a forester's hut somewhere back in this wilderness of pines, rushing streams, and lofty peaks, had driven a jeep over this track to and from the hotel's site. He had also mentioned that eventually the track curved to join the main highway.

But that had been two years ago, only weeks before the resort builder had abandoned his enterprise. Probably few if any vehicles had been this way since. Grass grew thickly on the crown of the road, and vines trailed across the ruts. In some places, winter freezing had heaved the knife-like edges of buried rocks through the track's surface. But he would get back to the highway somehow. He had to.

Chapter 20

Millard said, "Something is wrong. We should have heard gunfire by now."

The red-haired man behind the Volvo's wheel kept a discreet silence. About five minutes before, at Millard's order, he had stopped the car just a few feet short of where the narrow dirt road curved around a tall, treeless bluff of granite.

"Wait here," Millard said. "I'm going to see what the trouble is." He got out of the car, walked down the road, and disappeared around the granite bluff.

The short, sandy-haired man in the back seat said, "What do you think happened?"

"Who knows?" the driver said curtly. All day Millard had been hectoring him. "You're falling too far behind! —Don't let that truck get ahead of you!—No, don't get right behind them so soon again, you blockhead." As a result, the red-haired man was in a very bad humor.

"Do you think the Mercedes could have gone off the road and piled up in the valley?"

"Without our hearing the crash? Of course not."

"Maybe something went wrong with the plane. Maybe it never got here."

"Maybe you'd better shut your mouth." Just as Millard was senior to him, he was senior to the man in the back seat.

Minutes stretched out. There was silence except for

the keening sound of wind blowing down the valley. Then Millard reappeared around the granite bluff and trudged toward the car, his face red with exertion, or anger, or both. He got into the front seat, drew a few deep breaths, and then said, "The plane and the two men are there. The Mercedes is not."

The driver said cautiously, "What do you think—"

"I don't think it sprouted wings and flew! That damned Lescaut found some way off this road, probably through that little ravine back there."

"Shall I back up and—"

"No! We'd just be wasting our time. He would never have taken that route unless he had reason to think it would get him back to the highway. He may even have reached it by now."

Millard fell silent for a second or two, and then said, "Drive straight ahead to the site of that resort hotel. Turn around there, and go back to the highway. We'll try to pick up his trail."

The red-haired man started the Volvo. As he drove toward the curve ahead, he ventured one more question. "What did you tell the men who flew the plane in?"

"To go on waiting, of course, to fly their passenger to Budapest."

The Frenchman, Millard reflected, must be thinking by now that he would win. But he would not.

With relish, Millard recalled one of his recent chess games. His opponent, grown overconfident, had overlooked Millard's black bishop, lurking back there in the eighth rank. The bishop had swooped down and captured the white queen. Checkmate.

So it would be in Lescaut's case, because the Frenchman had more than overlooked a black bishop. He didn't even know the black bishop was on the board.

135

Chapter 21

The cart track had steepened, turning and twisting to follow the course of the narrow stream. Lescaut drove on through the artificial twilight created by the intermingled branches of the pines. Neither of the women had spoken, nor, for the last quarter of an hour, had he glanced into the mirror. But he could sense their apprehension.

He turned a curve, and then slowed almost to a halt. Ahead on the stream side of the track, the torrents of this or some other spring had torn a big chunk of earth away, so that for a stretch of about eight feet the track was only inches wider than the Mercedes itself. Aware of Manchester's angry, alarmed gaze, he drove forward.

Just before he reached the eroded stretch, he angled in as close to the mountainside as possible, and then speeded up. There was a metallic shriek as a jutting rock scraped the car's length. Then they were past the bad spot, and moving along a stretch that was not only sufficiently wide but comparatively level.

Muffy made a moaning sound. Lescaut looked into the mirror at his client's white face. "I am sorry, madame."

"You've always been such a careful driver!"

"I am sorry," he repeated. "It will be all right soon." And surely it would be. Surely soon this track would join the highway. And then, if he had really eluded Millard and his companions, if he could turn unhindered toward Salzburg and its airport, they would all be safe—his client, and the contemptuously angry young American beside him, and Joan, and perhaps even himself.

He looked at Joan's reflection. Her marvelous eyes were worried and a bit puzzled, but she smiled at him. He returned the smile and drove on.

Beyond the next curve he stopped abruptly. Probably weakened by its winter load of ice, a young poplar had toppled across the track. Its upper branches, their new leaves unfurled, lay trailing in the swift stream.

In a flat voice, Lescaut said to the man beside him, "You'll have to help me."

Not answering, Manchester opened the door and got out. He was silent for a few seconds as they approached the fallen tree. But when they were out of earshot of the women, he let out a few soft, fluent curses. "I thought that at least you knew your job. But this! First you leave the highway—as if it would have been any big deal to slow up for some construction!—and then you risk our lives on this cowpath."

Lescaut said, "No use to try to twist the tree from its stump. We will raise it upright and then try to lean it sidewise."

After that they worked in silence, first wading into icy water to lift the tree's crown onto a boulder at the stream's edge, and then heaving and straining until they had the slender trunk wedged in behind a pine tree. Still in silence, they returned to the car.

Muffy wailed, "You're both wet to the knees. Turn the heater up high, or you'll catch your deaths! We'll open the windows back here if it gets too hot."

"Thank you, madame."

He drove on, grateful for the blasts of warm air against

137

his wet trouser legs, and praying that each curve would not disclose another fallen tree, or eroded stretch, or—even worse—a boulder too large for two men to dislodge. He turned a final curve. And there, beyond a flat stretch of grassy meadow, cars and trucks streamed down the highway.

The track joined the main road about halfway between the roofed shrine and the ruined stone hut. Every nerve taut, he halted there for a few seconds and looked at the stream of oncoming cars. No black Volvo was visible. He joined the traffic, passed the ruined stone hut, and rounded the curve.

He heard his client say to Joan, "Will you pour me some water, dear? I had better take a migraine tablet."

He heard the click of the door to the little compartment which, set into the back of the front seat, held a water carafe and a glass. A few moments later his client said in a faint voice, "Mr. Lescaut, will you please stop someplace for tea? I don't feel well. All of that back there was very hard on my nerves."

"Yes, madame." She did not look well. Her mirrored face was very white, with a pinched look around the mouth.

His mind worked furiously. They would pass at least two restaurants before they turned off onto the road to Salzburg. He did not want to stop at either of them. He had no doubt that by now Millard was back on the highway again, trying to pick up his trail. He did not want to risk stopping anyplace, at least not until they were well on their way to Salzburg. And even then it would not be safe. They would not be safe until they were all aboard a plane for Paris, or Milan, or wherever the first plane out was headed.

138

He said, "I know of no restaurant nearby which serves anything at this hour, madame. But a bit farther along there is a restaurant run by a friend of mine. He will be glad to oblige you. Will that be all right, madame?"

"Yes." She leaned back in her corner and closed her eyes.

Lescaut drove on, over the high viaduct that spanned the U-shaped valley, and then around a series of curves. Although he kept looking in the mirror, and scanning the stream of traffic ahead whenever it curved to the left, he saw no black Volvo.

The turnoff to Salzburg was only a few miles ahead. He was sure that neither of the women would realize that they were not still headed for their scheduled overnight stop in Graz. But the chances were excellent that Manchester knew that Salzburg and Graz lay in different directions. From the corner of his eye he looked at the American's still-annoyed face. Manchester surely would demand explanations about the change of route. He might even demand to take over the driving. There would be a delay, a dangerous delay.

A road sign ahead. Even though it was not legible at that distance, Lescaut knew that it announced the Salzburg turnoff beyond it. He reached across Manchester, took a flashlight from the glove compartment, and let it fall to the car floor. "Could you get that for me, please?"

Not answering, Manchester bent over and groped with his right hand over the car floor. Unsuccessful, he twisted around and bent even farther, so that he could reach under the front seat. Lescaut speeded up, passed the sign, switched on the turn signal. "I can't find it," Manchester said in a muffled voice. "Oh, here it is."

He straightened. Lescaut followed a truck onto the

Salzburg turnoff. Manchester said, obviously irritated, "What do you want a flashlight for at four in the afternoon?"

"I just wanted to make sure it was there. The car has been in a garage for a week. Sometimes things are stolen."

From the American's expression, Lescaut gathered that Manchester, like Millard, suspected him of having gone on a drunken debauch his last night in Venice. He replaced the flashlight and then, with a slam, closed the glove compartment.

From the back seat Muffy said in a querulous tone he had never heard her use before, "You said the restaurant was not far."

"It is not more than another three miles, madame."

He had just completed a wide, looping curve. Looking to his left, he scanned the long stream of cars approaching the curve. His heart leaped. A black Volvo back there, separated from the Mercedes by perhaps a dozen vehicles. Millard's car? At that distance he could not tell. Speeding up, he passed a truck and turned the next curve. He could see the restaurant now. It stood off the highway, perhaps a hundred yards up the sloping mountainside, its sharply pitched Alpine roof visible above the pines.

Just beyond the restaurant's neat sign, announcing that luncheon was served from twelve until two and dinner from six until ten, he turned onto a graveled drive that sloped upward through a tunnel of tall pines. He was almost certain that Millard—if it was Millard back there—had not turned that last curve in time to see him leave the highway. Still, he did not stop at the restaurant's front entrance, where the Mercedes would be visible from the foot of the drive. Instead he drove past

140

the long porch, turned, and parked near the side door. "If you will wait for a moment, madame, I will make sure that the restaurant can accommodate you."

He went into the restaurant, letting the door close audibly behind him. The big room with its white-clothed tables, each decked with a bouquet of spring flowers, was empty. After a moment the bald, bearded proprietor, Heinrich Kranz, came through the swinging door from the kitchen. At this early hour he wore, not the formal evening clothes in which he greeted dinner guests, but corduroys and a blue shirt covered by a long white apron. "Why, Paul! It is good to see you."

The two men shook hands. Lescaut said, "Could you do me a favor? Could my client—she is an elderly lady —and the two people with her have tea, and perhaps sandwiches if they are hungry?"

Already Heinrich was whipping off his apron. "For you, anything." Paul had brought him thousands of dollars' worth of business over the years.

"And would you mind if I ran my car into your garage? I may have to change a tire."

"Please do. Use any of my tools that you need."

Lescaut went out to the car. "It is all right, madame." He handed his client down to the graveled parking space, and then Joan. Before he could stop himself, he tightened his hand around hers. The faint, puzzled worry was still in her eyes, but her smile was warm. He heard the slam of the car door on Manchester's side, and released Joan's hand. Just before the American hurried ahead to open the restaurant door, Lescaut caught a glimpse of his lowering face. Was he still angry because of that dangerous ride over the cart track? Or had that lingering handclasp aroused his jealousy? If only you knew, Lescaut thought, how hard I am working to save your neck, all our necks.

The garage's overhead door was up. He drove into the shadowy interior and parked in the vacant space beyond Heinrich's sporty red Porsche and Frau Kranz's blue Buick station wagon. As he had feared, his left rear tire and his right front one were both a little soft. Doubtless they had been cut on the sharp rocks knifing through the ruts. Both leaks, though, obviously were slow ones. Should he change the softer tire? No, best not to take the time. He wanted to be ready to move on toward Salzburg the moment his party emerged from the restaurant. If he filled both tires with air, they would last for at least fifty miles, and probably more.

With his own jack he raised the front tire and, using the old hand pump which had hung on this garage wall as long as he had been coming here, filled the tire with air. Then, carrying the jack and the pump, he moved to the car's rear.

He was replacing the cap on the air valve of the jacked-up rear tire when he became aware of movement behind him. Before he could look around, something struck him on the back of the head. He felt blinding pain, and then, for an interval, nothing at all.

Chapter 22

"Mein Herr?" It was a child's voice.

Lescaut opened his eyes and found that he was lying on the garage floor, left cheek against the cold cement. Near him stood a pair of legs in knee socks and gray woolen shorts. He forced his blurred gaze upward, and saw that it was Heinrich's blond ten-year-old son who stood there, blue eyes alarmed. "Are you ill, mein Herr?"

Aware of the agonizing throb in his head, Lescaut sat up. "Yes. Go in the restaurant and tell the American gentleman that I must see him. Don't say anything else to anyone. Will you do that?"

The boy nodded and turned away. Lescaut heard his feet running over the gravel. Painfully, he stood up and leaned against the side of the Mercedes. His hand, gingerly touching the back of his head, came away unbloodied. No cut, and probably no skull fracture. At least a slight concussion, though. Otherwise, surely, the pain would not be this bad.

The slam of the restaurant's side door, and the crunch of footsteps over gravel. Turning his head, Lescaut tried to focus his blurred gaze on Manchester's face.

Manchester asked sharply, "What the hell happened to you?"

"Someone hit me over the head. But never mind that. You will have to drive. Take the jack away, and then go get the women. Drive us to the airport at Salzburg."

"Salzburg! Why, we're going to—"

"Listen to me. Watch out for a black Volvo with three men in it. They plan to kidnap her." He knew he should be thinking better, explaining this better, but he was in too much pain.

"Kidnap! Joan?"

Lescaut shook his head, and then wished he had not.

"You mean Muffy? Why would anyone want to—"

"Because she is who she is—was. They are Russians. I think they want to use her to create some sort of crisis. I think—" He struggled to frame another sentence, and then gave up. "You see?"

Even to Lescaut's blurred gaze, the young American's face was a study in incredulity. He said in a flat voice, "I think you're crazy. Even if all that were true, how would you know about it?"

Lescaut saw that he would have to say it. "Because I have been in Russian pay for the last ten years."

Manchester was silent for perhaps three seconds, and then said, "You've been *what?*"

"Now will you believe me about the men in the Volvo?"

Manchester's voice was very cold. "If you are what you say you are, why should I believe anything else you tell me?"

Lescaut said desperately, "They plan to kill the rest of us. Take the old lady away in a plane, and then kill us. That is why I drove over that cart track. I was trying to get away from them. Why else should I have risked wrecking the car?"

Manchester said nothing.

"I thought I had gotten away from them, but they are around here someplace. It is up to you now to try to get

144

us aboard the first plane out of Salzburg, and then on a plane to New York."

Manchester's lips twisted. "New York! *You* want to go to America, after what you've just told me? What do you think will happen to you there?"

"I—I don't know. I have been hoping—" He broke off. He wanted to say that he had hoped that the Americans, because of what he had tried to do today, would take him in and perhaps even let him stay there. But the thought was too complex for his throbbing brain to form into words.

When Manchester spoke, it was still in that cold voice. But his words filled Lescaut with overwhelming relief. "All right, I'll go along with it. Maybe I'm a fool, but I'm going to believe that you are telling the truth." He paused. "Shall I tell the women all this?"

"No! They might panic and insist on staying here and calling the police. And before the police got here—"

"All right. I'll tell them you slipped on some grease and struck your head, and that we'd better take you to the hospital in Salzburg."

"Yes." Thank God Manchester could think. He himself could not.

"Get in the front seat. I'll take the jack away, and then go get the women."

Sitting with closed eyes beside the driver's seat, Lescaut winced as the car's right rear tire struck the cement, winced again as Manchester tossed the jack into the trunk. Then he heard the crunch of withdrawing footsteps.

Minutes later he heard the footsteps return. He opened his eyes. Manchester appeared on Lescaut's side of the car, a paper cup of water in one hand and a vial of small white pills in the other. With an effort, Lescaut

145

rolled the window down.

Manchester handed Lescaut the water, and then shook two pills into the Frenchman's other palm. "Migraine pills, from Muffy. If they can kill migraine, they ought to do at least something for a guy who's been slugged."

Gratefully, Lescaut swallowed the pills. "Where are—"

"I see them coming out of the restaurant now."

Lescaut leaned back in his corner of the front seat, dimly aware of the engine's steady hum. Before his mind's vision Joan's face seemed to float, looking as it had when she stood beside him there in the garage—very white, with a terrible anxiety in her wide-set eyes. Sorry for her anxiety, and yet gratified by it, he had tried to smile at her before his eyelids closed.

Those pills were good. They had muted the pain to a dull throb, and left him suspended somewhere between sleep and waking, so that he could not have said whether they had left the restaurant fifteen minutes ago or several times that. All sound seemed to come from far away, including the conversation in the car. There was little of it. They were keeping quiet for his sake. Once he had heard Joan ask, "Are you sure this is the right way?" and had heard Manchester answer, "Yes."

Another time he had heard Muffy's voice. "He must be asleep, poor man. How many pills did you give him?"

"Two."

"I said one."

"I'm sorry. I thought you said two."

"Well, they won't hurt him, I suppose. They'll just make him sleep. And perhaps that's the best thing for him now."

He had not opened his eyes then, or since, lest the light

reawaken the mind-crippling pain. Perhaps soon he would be himself again, able to help if Manchester needed him. In the meantime, it was all up to Manchester.

Something bothered him, though—something that had not occurred to his befuddled brain until now. Millard or some of his men obviously had been close by back there at the restaurant. Why were they allowing Manchester to slip away, unchallenged, toward Salzburg? His mind fumbled with the problem for a moment, and then slid toward sleep.

Chapter 23

Manchester looked into the rear-view mirror. Both women were leaning back, each in her corner, with closed eyes. He felt sure, though, that only the old lady napped. The girl's tense face was not that of a sleeper. A lovely girl, Joan. For perhaps the hundredth time, he wished that she was not so lovely.

He wondered if his mother, if she had lived, would in time have come to look like Muffy. A little, perhaps. His mother, too, had been delicate of feature, with a slightly tilted nose that had given her, even in middle age, a childlike appearance. And his mother, too, toward the last, had been plump, but not from food.

How old had he been when he discovered what his father and the servants meant when they told him that his mother was "too ill" to see him? Twelve? Something like that, although her heavy drinking must have started some years earlier.

All through prep school he had suspected that her drinking had something to do with his father, or, more specifically, his father's women. Dan Manchester could not remember a time, from early childhood on, when he had not disliked and feared his father. Daniel Manchester, Senior, that big, loud-voiced man, ordering him to "stop blubbering like a girl" when, at the age of four, he had cried over a puppy's death. Manchester, Senior,

148

snatching an A. A. Milne book from his hands when he was six, and telling him to go out and get some exercise. "No son of mine is going to grow up into a poetry-reading nance."

Still, the self-righteous, flag-waving old bastard must have made his wife fairly happy for the first seven or eight years of their married life. Otherwise she could not have made her son so happy. And during his early childhood Dan had been happy with her, especially when, as often happened, his father was absent from the estate near Stamford, Connecticut. He remembered the joy of dining alone with his brown-haired mother, so pretty and slender in those days, or driving with her in the wicker cart drawn by a piebald pony named Bubbles.

His mother died when he was in his junior year at Yale. "Her heart gave out," his father had told him over the phone. As he drove from New Haven to Stamford, Dan had wondered bitterly if it had not been sleeping pills, plus a liberal quantity of alcohol. It was not her own doctor, but one of her husband's choosing, who had been called in to write the death certificate.

Two days after his mother's funeral, while going through the books in her room, Dan had found her diary. Not until then was he aware of the extent of his mother's past misery and his father's cruelty. With fury and still-raw grief, he read of the times his father had brought home "a new secretary" for the weekend. Under threat that her liquor supply would be cut off, his wife had been forced to sit at the dinner table with him and his latest floozy. Later, in her room, she had downed bourbon until she could no longer hear the sounds coming from her husband's room across the hall.

There were other cruelties. An entry dated two weeks before her death told of how her youngest and favorite sister had telephoned, without her knowing about it, to say that she was coming for a visit. Her husband had brought the sister upstairs to where Dan's mother lay sodden with drink. He had stood in the doorway, smiling at the shock in the sister's face and at his wife's clumsy struggles to sit up.

Dan had burned the diary. He had never mentioned it to his father, nor to anyone else. He had gone back to Yale and played football so competently—always ironically aware of his old man cheering up there somewhere in the stands—that he had been named all–Ivy League defensive end.

His next summer vacation he had gone to Europe, lingering for two months in Czechoslovakia. He had made friends of several Communist Party members, students of about his own age, and their older associates. Seated with them in cafés night after night, he had expressed freely his dislike of his father. And in terms even more scathing than those used by his companions, he had denounced the policies, both foreign and domestic, of his own country.

At last he received a phone call from a stranger who mentioned mutual friends. He met the man in a Prague public park for what turned out to be the first of a series of long talks.

At the end of the summer he had returned to Yale, completed his senior year, and then, as the man in Prague had instructed him to do, applied for a job with the CIA. The CIA had no openings just then, but, after an interval, he was able to join the Secret Service. It always amused him to think that his father's influence had expedited his appointment.

Since then he had moved very carefully. He had cultivated his superiors. He had impressed them by work-

150

ing hard even when off duty, supplementing his college French with advanced studies, and learning elementary German and Russian. He had made himself agreeable to whatever VIP he was assigned to as a bodyguard. And he had waited for the chance to be useful to his friends abroad.

The chance had come. It mattered little to Manchester that it was an opposition faction within the Soviet spy apparatus which had gotten in touch with him. Nor did he care that, in the long run, the old lady's kidnaping would strengthen the hand of diehard Russia haters like his father. In the short run his father, reading or listening to her sorrowful denunciation of her dead husband and his advisers, would be apoplectic with impotent fury.

And the best part of it was that Dan himself would return to America, and to his job, as a hero—a hero who had been wounded—only slightly, but still wounded—in his attempt to save the presidential widow. There would be no one to contradict his story, because after the plane took off with the old lady inside, he would use the gun. Not his own gun, but a rifle the two Russians in the plane would leave behind.

Joan. Joan was the bad part. If only she had gone home after one of Millard's men knocked her down on that street in Florence. But she had not, and later on, in Venice, Millard somehow again had failed, so that now he himself was left with a task for which he had no stomach whatsoever.

He thought of that brief telephone conversation with Millard in Venice the night before. He'd had to keep reminding himself that Millard was his superior. Otherwise he might have used on the KGB man his limited but forceful supply of Russian curse words.

Well, no point in thinking about that. Think about the plane. It would still be there. Millard would have had enough confidence in him—confidence that somehow he would get the old lady and the others to the landing strip —to tell the two men with the plane to wait.

His thoughts veered to something that some writer— was it Rebecca West?—had written about those who betray their country. A traitor, the writer said, was often someone who identified his country with a bitterly hated father. When he had read that he had felt a shock of self-recognition. Then he had thought, smiling, "Right on, sister."

Speeding up, he passed three cars, moved back into his own lane, and then glanced at Lescaut, slumped beside him with his head lolling against the seat back. The double-crossing jerk. That wild ride over that rutted track, and then, just before the Salzburg turnoff, that cute bit with the flashlight.

With amusement, Manchester thought of how easy it had been back at the restaurant. Saying that he wanted to consult a guidebook he had left in the car, he had gone out the side door. Almost immediately, hearing the wheeze of the old tire pump, he had known that he was in luck. The noise would cover the sound of his approach. He had hurried across the gravel and slipped into the garage beside a blue station wagon. A heavy wrench hung on the wall. He took it down. Wrench in hand, he had crept up on the kneeling man.

Well, he had been warned to watch Lescaut carefully, lest he try something at the last minute. He himself knew little about the Frenchman except that he had been in Russian pay for quite a while, carrying messages from one city to another, and being kept on ice until he was really needed.

152

They had been fools, Manchester thought contemptuously, to depend at all upon the Frenchman. When the chips were down in this line of work, you could not expect a man to risk his freedom or his life solely for money. To be willing to do that, a man had to hate.

✤

Chapter 24

Joan's voice, sharp to the point of anger, brought Lescaut up through layers of drowsiness. "Now I know you've taken the wrong route! Why, we're headed back the way we came. I remember this bridge."

Bridge? Yes, they must be crossing a bridge, a long high one. He could hear that peculiar slat-slat sound made by air rushing between the uprights of a viaduct's guard rail.

Manchester said, "You're mistaken. It just looks something like the other one."

The slat-slat sound ceased. Now there was just the hum of the engine. Should he, Lescaut wondered, risk opening his eyes to the stab of light? His mind felt clearer now, much clearer. But he knew that the sickening pain still lurked.

The car turned left. He could hear dirt spewing from beneath the tires. Then the car hit a bump that awoke a preliminary throb in his head. This time it was his client who spoke. "Dan! What are you doing? This is the same awful road we were on three hours ago!"

Sudden surmise held Lescaut frozen for a moment. Then he opened his eyes a slit. With a sense of being in the grip of a nightmare, he saw that they were indeed right back where they had been in midafternoon, not long before that wild ride over the cart track. The light

154

of the declining sun behind him showed him the narrow dirt road, the steep mountainside on the right, the U-shaped valley on the left.

Instinct, as well as shock, held him silent and motionless, eyelids almost closed. Of course, he thought. If his brain had been in working order, instead of crippled first by a blow and then by a double dose of analgesic, he would have realized almost at once the significance of their unimpeded flight from the restaurant. It must have been Manchester who had struck him down, not Millard or one of his men.

Probably Millard and his companions had been nowhere near the restaurant. It had been someone else's black Volvo he had seen approaching that wide, looping curve.

But then where were Millard and his men now? Cruising up and down the highway, trying to spot the Mercedes? Or had they already spotted it? Perhaps right now the Volvo and its occupants, all of them no doubt armed, was only a few curves behind them on this dirt road.

But if that were the case, he had no chance at all, and so he must not let himself think that the Volvo was back there. He must think about what awaited them at the end of this road. He still sat motionless, mind working furiously, and only dimly aware of the renewed throbbing in his head.

Joan's voice was really angry now. "Dan! Why are we on this road?"

"All right." Manchester sounded shamefaced. "I didn't want to admit that I'd goofed, but I guess I'll have to. We were going the wrong way back there on the highway. Lescaut said we'd make better time on this road, so I've taken it."

"But that was *before*." Bewildered anxiety in Muffy's

155

voice. "Before his accident, I mean. We were headed for Graz then. Now we've got to get that poor man to the hospital in Salzburg. And anyway, there's a rock slide on this road. He saw the sign."

"I didn't see any sign, and I'll bet neither of you did, either. There was something wrong with the guy even before he slipped and—"

The Mercedes' horn blared. "Damn! That was an accident. Look, ladies, do you mind keeping quiet? If I make a mistake, we're apt to end up on the valley floor."

Yes, Lescaut thought, and if he himself tried to wrest control of the car from Manchester, they were apt to end up on the valley floor. From the corner of his eye he looked down at the space between himself and Manchester on the leather seat. If the flight bag had been there, he might have been able to snatch the gun out and force Manchester to stop. But he saw that the big American, taking no chances, had placed the bag on the car floor beneath his knees.

That still left the Mauser. He would just have to hope that when the time came, he would be able to grab the Mauser from its clip under the instrument panel.

If the Mauser was still there. Lescaut felt sweat roll down his side. Perhaps it was not. Perhaps, when Manchester retrieved the flashlight from the car floor, he had seen the gun in its clip. But no, probably not. The car had been climbing a slight grade then. The flashlight had rolled, not forward under the instrument panel, but backward toward the seat.

He could see the prow-like bluff now, no longer gray, but tawny in the light of the descending sun. Only a minute or so left. Sure that Manchester threw a glance at him from time to time, he still sat motionless with head lolled back, eyes barely open.

156

The car followed the curve around the tall bluff. Lescaut let his head roll to one side and then, as the car straightened, roll back again. They turned a second curve, a third. There it was, what he had been almost sure he would see—the light plane on the landing strip in the valley, the roofless stone walls of that never-completed hotel on the mountainside at the valley's eastern end, and, standing on either side of the road, two men in dark trousers and brown leather jackets. The blond, short man who stood on the valley side of the road carried a light machine gun. The other one, darker-haired and taller, held a leveled rifle.

"What in God's name—" Manchester braked the car to a stop. Lescaut heard Joan's sharp intake of breath and her cousin's whimpering cry.

The man with the rifle stepped to the center of the road and called in heavily accented English, "We know you have a gun. Throw it out of the car."

"Joan! Get down," Manchester said. "Both of you, get down. If he lets go with that machine gun—"

"Throw your gun out!" the man with the rifle yelled. "Then both men are to get out of the car with hands raised."

Manchester opened the car door and kicked the flight bag to the side of the road. Hands in the air, he said sharply, "Lescaut! Can you hear me? They want us both out." He stepped to the road. The flight bag with the gun in it was still too close to the car. With his foot he sent it skidding across the road to lodge against a pine seedling at the cliff's edge. Then he waited until the Frenchman, apparently too dazed to open the door on his side of the car, slid under the wheel and then stood leaning against the Mercedes, hands raised barely to shoulder height.

Manchester moved then, hands still in the air, toward the two armed men. His stomach had knotted up. He had been told that the man with the rifle was a top marksman, the very best available. But now and then even a top marksman—

"Hey!" he called. "What is this?"

The rifle cracked. Manchester spun to his left under the bullet's impact, staggered a few feet, and fell to the road. The guy was good, all right. Manchester had felt, not the numbing slam of a bullet against bone, but only a burning sensation in the fleshiest part of his upper left arm.

All he had to do was to lie here for a few more moments, a fallen hero in the old lady's eyes. Then the rifleman, moving past him toward the car, would drop his rifle onto the road. He and the man with the machine gun would force the old lady to start down the slope.

Left alone with an unarmed, semi-conscious man and a girl, Manchester would get to his feet, pick up the Russian rifle, and walk toward them.

That was the way it would be, he thought bleakly, because that was the way it had to be.

Chapter 25

When he saw Manchester stagger and then fall to the road, Lescaut had not allowed himself time to wonder why the rifleman should have shot an obvious co-conspirator. As if too weak to stand, he let his hands drop and his body sag lower against the car's side. Behind the shelter of the opened car door, his hand darted under the instrument panel. Aware that in a split second a bullet or bullets might slam into his head, or through the door's glass upper part into his body, he grasped the Mauser and drew it from its clip.

The machine gunner first. Swiftly he lifted the gun and fired over the door's upper edge. As he ducked down behind the door, he caught a glimpse through the glass of the man staggering toward the road's lip. He heard the impact of machine gun bullets against the car's hood. The man must have been firing convulsively, because the weapon still chattered for a second or two even after Lescaut knew, from the direction of the sound, that the machine gunner had plunged down the steep slope.

A rifle bullet slammed into the Mercedes' steel door. Lescaut dropped to his knees and stretched out on his stomach in the dirt. He fired past Manchester's still figure at the Russian's legs, and saw him crumple, with the rifle slithering from his hands.

A wave of giddiness struck Lescaut. For a moment

there seemed to be a gray mist in front of his eyes. He heard Joan scream, "Paul! Look out!" and heard the rear door open and footsteps run across the road.

He shook his head to clear the mist away, and saw that the rifle no longer lay in the road. Manchester must have gotten to his feet and scooped up the weapon, because now he lay prone in the dirt, aiming the rifle under the door at Lescaut's head. Lescaut fired, missed, and felt a rifle bullet slam into his right shoulder. The Mauser dropped from his paralyzed hand. He twisted around, put his left hand on the floor of the car, and tried to hoist himself up so he would be shielded by the door.

Movement beside him. A pistol fired, above him and a little to his right. Then he heard something strike the dirt close beside him. He looked at it. It was a thirty-eight, from that flight bag Manchester had kicked to the roadside.

He looked up at Joan, standing there ashen-faced, eyes wide with horror. "I think he's— I think I—"

He managed to get to his feet, aware that not only his shoulder but his whole right side felt numb. One look at Manchester's head, as he lay there in the road, hands still fastened on the rifle, told Lescaut that she was right. He was dead, killed by a bullet from his own gun.

But the rifleman was alive. With his right leg dragging behind him, he crawled on both hands and one knee toward that rifle in Manchester's dead hands. "Stop!" Lescaut yelled. "Stop right there." He stooped and picked up the Mauser in his left hand.

The rifleman kept up that labored crawl. Fleetingly, Lescaut found something admirable in the other man's determination. But he was almost within arm's reach of the rifle now. Aware that with his left hand he might very well miss, Lescaut steadied the gun's barrel on the upper edge of the car door, and took careful aim. He fired, and the crawling figure slumped to the dirt.

With a brief glance at Manchester, Lescaut walked over to the Russian. The bullet had gone through his neck. Aware now of blood running from his left shoulder down to his wrist, he walked back to where Joan stood, that dazed horror still in her face. Her gaze dropped to his right hand. "There's blood on your hand. Are—are you—"

Not answering, he bent his head and looked inside the car at his client. She lay across the seat, eyes closed. He reached for the plump wrist. There was a pulse, faint and erratic, but still a pulse.

Her eyelids fluttered open. "What—what—"

"It is all right," he said. "Just stay there. Just rest."

He straightened and looked around. Joan had disappeared. Then he heard her, over there behind a roadside boulder, being violently sick. After perhaps a minute she walked back to him. She said in a toneless voice, "I never dreamed that I could— I mean, I never even fired a gun before."

"I know how you must feel. But if you had not done it, we would all be dead by now." Yes, all of them, even the President's widow, would have been dead, killed by bullets from a Russian rifle. With the kidnap attempt blocked, Manchester would not have wanted anyone left alive to contradict his version of what had happened in this valley today.

Joan said, "Take off your jacket and shirt. We've got to stop the bleeding."

He shook his head. "Later. Just give me something to hold over the wound. I must make sure about the man with the machine gun."

Not arguing, she took the green scarf from her coat

pocket. He wadded it up and thrust it under his shirt, over the wound. Then he walked about thirty yards down the road and looked over the edge.

He saw the machine gunner immediately, but not his weapon. It must have slid farther down the precipitous slope. The man himself, apparently, had rolled over and over until, about twenty feet down the slope, the trunk of a dead pine had arrested his descent. He lay with sightless eyes staring up at the sunset-flushed sky.

Lescaut turned away. Death could come so quickly. How much time had elapsed since Manchester, hands raised, had stepped from the car onto the road? Five minutes? Not much more than that.

As he moved back toward the Mercedes, he became aware that his head still ached. His shoulder ached too, now that the numbness had worn off. The bullet had not gone through. If it had, he would have felt a trickle of blood down his back. Well, a bullet lodged in his shoulder would not kill him. It was going to hurt like hell until someone took it out, but it would not kill him. He took his left hand away from his shoulder. The scarf, stuck fast to the wound now, stayed in place.

When he reached the car, Joan said, "Is the man with the machine gun—"

He nodded.

She reached toward him. "Let me help you take off—"

"No. The bleeding's stopped. Best to leave it alone for now. We must try to get out of here." He walked to the front of the Mercedes. At least a dozen machine gun bullets had torn into its grill. There was almost no chance that the engine would run. But if it would, they could drive up to that half-finished hotel, turn around, and drive back to the highway before darkness closed down. He said, "Will you try to start the car?"

She got behind the wheel, switched on the ignition, stepped on the starter. There was no response. She said, her face pale in the fading light. "What shall we do?"

He was silent. What could they do? His client, now crying softly there in the back seat, would never be able to walk ten miles back to the highway. For that matter he knew that he, weak from loss of blood now, would never make it. Send Joan? Not when there still was a good chance that Millard and his men would return here. He pictured her alone on the road, with the Volvo's headlights bearing down upon her.

The plane. He could fly a plane, but not with one arm. And even with two arms, and even in full daylight, it would be hard enough to lift a plane off a broken runway, and then fly it over these mountains.

He tried to make his voice light. "You are not an expert pilot by any chance, are you?"

With a faint smile, she shook her head.

"Then we had better take both lap robes—there is an extra one in the trunk—and walk back to where that track turns off beside the stream. We can hide back there until daylight." He hesitated, and then added, "You see, there are more of them than just Manchester and those two gunmen. They probably will come here." His own words filled him with a sense of urgency, a feeling that at any moment he might hear the whine of the Volvo's engine.

Her face had gone even paler. But all she said was, "I can carry the blankets, and help Muffy. But the guns. Shouldn't we—"

"I'll carry the Mauser and the thirty-eight in the flight bag."

In that moment he realized he more than just loved her. He was so very proud of her. She could not help but be filled with questions. And yet because she knew that he had no extra strength to spend, she had asked none of them.

Soon, though, he would have to answer those questions, including the one about his own part in all this. And then what would he see in her face?

For a moment a paralyzing bleakness settled over him. Then he walked to the car's open rear door and said to his client, "We must leave the car, madame, and walk a little way back up the road."

Muffy raised a tear-wet, crumpled face. "Why has all this happened? Why—why, it's like a nightmare."

Joan had gotten out of the car to stand beside him. "Don't!" she said, her voice sharp. "Don't waste time with questions, Muffy. Just get out of the car, darling."

A few minutes later they moved up the road through the thickening dark, Joan with one arm around her elderly relative and the other laden not only with two lap robes, but a heavy overcoat she had taken from Lescaut's duffel bag. Walking beside the two women, Lescaut realized with something like panic that he was so weak that even the two guns and the flashlight in the small flight bag seemed to drag at his one good arm.

Chapter 26

"I learned of this less than an hour ago, Mr. President."
The voice of the interpreter, traveling across eight thousand miles of mountain and plain and ocean, was agitated—almost as agitated as the Russian voice whose words he had just put into English.

The big man standing beside his desk, telephone held to his ear, ran fingers through his sparse and already rumpled hair. What time was it in Moscow? Since it was a little past noon here, it must be past eight at night there. He asked, "And you have no idea where she is?" The tall young man standing on the other side of the desk, with a second phone in his hand, translated the question into Russian.

"We have some idea, Mr. President. Brodsky, the Poliburo member who informed me of the conspiracy, said the lady was to be kidnaped somewhere in the eastern Austrian Alps and flown to Budapest."

"And then?" Because the day was cloudy, lights had been turned on at various spots in the spacious office. He could see his dim reflection in one of the long windows, an incongruous reflection of a big man in a gray flannel sweatsuit. He had been down in the gymnasium, trying to work off that extra inch around his middle, when word came that the Chairman was on the line.

"Brodsky says the plan was to keep her imprisoned in

a house outside of Budapest for as many days as necessary, and then present her to the world as—as someone who had decided to defect. She was to broadcast statements about her late husband and his advisers that—that would be highly embarrassing to both our governments. In fact—"

The translator's voice broke off. After a moment the man in the sweatsuit said grimly, "In fact, they hoped we would be right back where we have been for a generation —glaring at each other over piles of missiles that kept getting higher and higher."

"And with neither of our countries feeling any the safer for it. Exactly, Mr. President. Now we shall inform the Austrian government. They will, I am sure, put search planes in the air. And Budapest police will be searching the city and its environs, in case she has already been flown over the Hungarian border. As for the handful of conspirators in the Politburo, rest assured that I have ordered their arrest."

"I never doubted it," the big man said dryly.

Muffy, he thought. Muffy, of all people. When his campaign trail had taken him through Cleveland the previous summer, he had paid a courtesy visit to that most self-effacing of ex–First Ladies. She had talked then of how she might "do" Europe in the spring. And only last week his wife had mentioned receiving a letter from her, mailed from Italy.

He had known, even before he was sworn into office, that the years ahead would hold, not only predictable problems and dangers, but unforeseen ones too. It had never occurred to him, though, that Muffy, plump, gentle little Muffy, would fall victim to a bunch of hard-lining Russians. He said, "I assume a Secret Service man was with her. Was there anyone else?"

"A younger woman. Not a daughter. Brodsky, who has been under extreme nervous strain, cannot remember whether she is a niece or a cousin. And there is a courier, a Frenchman. It was Brodsky's impression that Karpolovich, the ringleader of the conspiracy, believed that the Frenchman could be pressured into a certain amount of cooperation, but was not sure of it."

"I see." Best not to mention in his first news conference that the French courier might be in on it. Things were going to be sticky enough for the next few hours without agitated calls from the French Embassy. "Does Brodsky know what was to happen to the young woman and the Secret Service man and the courier?"

The reply was several seconds in coming. "Brodsky is not sure. He has the impression that Karpolovich has been withholding some of the truth from him. He fears that the real plan is to kill all three of the lady's companions."

God! A Presidential widow in Russian hands, and three others, including an American Secret Service man, dead by Russian bullets. And he had just remembered something else his wife had told him. Muffy's letter had mentioned that her bodyguard was old Dan Manchester's son—old Dan, that most bellicose of the Russia haters.

He thought of the hotheads in Congress, each trying to sound more belligerent than his likeminded colleagues. He thought of mass meetings called by people like Manchester, meetings that would attract not only those who had been opposed to detente all along, but thousands of others as well. He thought of tens of thousands of wires and phone calls which would soon deluge the White House, many of them demanding that Washington "do something"—such as wipe Russia off the map immediately with nuclear bombs.

"Now I know, Mr. President, that we Russians have a reputation for secrecy. We like to, as you Americans say, play our cards close to— Is it the nose?"

"The vest, Mr. Chairman, the vest." Despite his anxiety, the big man smiled.

"Quite so. But in this case I think that secrecy would be disastrous. The longer this is kept from the world, the more chance that your people will believe that this has been an act of the Russian government, instead of just a few rash men."

"I concur. In fact, I was about to tell you that I intend to call a press conference as soon as we finish this conversation."

"Good. I will keep you constantly informed of all developments. And you will do the same for me?"

"Yes."

"Then good-bye, Mr. President."

"Good-bye."

He put the phone in its cradle and just stood there for a moment, hand pressing down on the instrument. Then he looked at the young interpreter. "I've got to go and get dressed. Will you call my press secretary immediately and ask him to come here?"

Chapter 27

Lescaut awoke sometime during the night, aware that his shoulder felt not only painful, but feverish. He had an impulse to unbutton his overcoat. But no. Even though he felt uncomfortably warm, he knew that the night must be chill, perhaps only a few degrees above freezing. And the pine-branch mattress upon which he lay was little protection against the deepr cold striking up through the earth.

The half moon was still up. Its light filtered down through the trees onto this little grassy clearing, about ten feet above the car track, to which they had climbed. On the opposite side of the open space he could see two dark mounds—his client and Joan, each wrapped in a lap robe.

He listened. No sound except the chatter of the stream. On this windless night, not even the trees were stirring. His shoulder felt even hotter now. The thought of blood poisoning crossed his mind. No use to speculate about that. He and Joan had taken every precaution which was possible under the circumstances. Even before they cut branches for three pine mattresses—with Joan holding the feathery tip of each branch, his client holding the flashlight, and he sawing laboriously away with a pocket knife held in his one good hand—even before that his shoulder had been tended. Beside the stream, Joan had helped him off with his jacket and shirt, soaked the blood-stiffened scarf from his shoulder and bathed the wound. One of several clean pocket handkerchiefs, which Joan had taken from his duffel bag along with his overcoat, had served as a bandage.

No, he would not get blood poisoning. Most wounds felt feverish for a while. By daylight, he would be much better, well enough to walk the ten miles to the highway.

And after that? Well, soon after that he would be arrested. But before that happened, he would have to steel himself for that look he knew would be on Joan's face, and tell her the truth about himself.

Sleep, he commanded himself. You've got to sleep. After a while his mind blurred, and he slid toward unconsciousness.

Staring into the dim moonlight, Joan saw Muffy stir and then turn over on her back in the lap robe cocoon. Thank God she could sleep. Anxious as she was for Paul, Joan had worried about her elderly relative, too. But Muffy, for all her gentle and even frivolous exterior, came from tough pioneer stock. After that one fit of hysterical weeping back there at the car, she had behaved with fortitude. She had not wept, or complained, or asked questions about the two gunmen who had confronted them on the road, or anything else.

Those two men. They had been Russians. They had looked like Russians. The one with the rifle had spoken with a Russian accent. And they had not been ordinary holdup men. Something far more important than robbery was involved. The presence of the little plane down there in the valley attested to that. And the way Dan Manchester had taken the Russian's rifle and turned it

170

upon those he was supposed to protect attested to it doubly.

Dan Manchester's head, after the bullet struck. She blotted out the picture. She'd had to do it. He would have killed Paul, and then perhaps, as Paul had said, Muffy and herself. She could still see his face as he lay there with the rifle at his shoulder, his skin white and drawn taut over the cheekbones, his blue eyes blazing. Without ever having seen a killer's face before, she had known in that moment that Dan Manchester's was such a face.

Paul muttered something. Perhaps he was feverish. She fought down the desire to cross the clearing and touch his face. Best not to risk waking him. And it was both futile and foolish for her to keep worrying about blood poisoning. Why, she had heard of people walking around for years with bits of metal—bullets or pieces of shrapnel—lodged in their bodies. Besides, there were all kinds of drugs with which to fight infection. When he reached a hospital, and surely they would manage that soon, he would be all right.

But he would need food. And she needed something in which to carry water up from the stream. In spite of those two still figures lying there in the road, as soon as it grew light she would slip down to the car. Muffy had left an unopened box of Perugia chocolates there. She had bought them that morning—how long ago that seemed!—before they left Venice. She would bring the chocolates and the water carafe back with her. And if she saw no sign of danger down there, she would try to get a news broadcast on the car radio.

Danger. Paul had said there was still danger. He had said there were men who might come looking for them.

Where were those men now? She strained her ears to listen. No sound of a car coming down that dirt road along the mountainside. No sound at all but that of the rushing stream.

How did Paul know that men might come looking for them?

Her mind shrank away from the question. Sleep, she told herself. You must sleep.

Chapter 28

Under the blue-white glare of the fluorescent light, the garageman closed the Volvo's battered hood. "I cannot repair it, mein Herr. You will need a new tie rod, and I must send to Villoch for that."

Millard, whose German was poor, asked the garageman to repeat his words. Then he turned and glared at the red-haired man who sat, shoulders hunched, on a bench against the garage wall. The sandy-haired man beside him, as if to disassociate himself from the unfortunate driver, stared at a grease spot on the floor.

The accident had happened about four hours earlier, while they were searching up and down the highway for the Mercedes. Rounding a curve too fast, the Volvo had slammed into a guardrail. Fortunately it had not bounced back into the stream of oncoming cars. But the Volvo had been forced to wait there until a patrol car stopped, and then wait even longer until a tow truck arrived. Then the car had been drawn, front end hoisted in the air, to this garage in a town only a few miles north of the Italian border.

It is not my fault, the driver thought. For almost twelve hours now, ever since nine that morning, he'd had to swallow his resentment of Millard's constant heckling. Subjected to such long torment, any driver might make a mistake.

Millard turned back to the garageman and asked in his atrocious German if there was a car rental agency nearby.

"No, mein Herr. There is one in a town fifteen miles to the east, but it closes at five each day."

Millard looked at the gray Citroen standing against the garage's opposite wall. "Then rent me your car for a few hours. I will pay you well."

The Austrian looked at the Volvo's mashed-in radiator. "I am sorry, but I never let anyone else drive my car. Why not stay tonight at the inn here, and telephone the car rental people in the morning?"

Millard had an impulse to reach inside his jacket to his shoulder holster and demand, at gunpoint, that the Citroen be turned over to him. But he realized that would be a foolish act indeed. If, thanks to Manchester, the seizure of the widow had been accomplished as planned, there was no urgent need for Millard himself to drive down into the valley tonight. On the other hand, if Manchester had failed, if that damned Frenchman had somehow managed to defeat him— Well, in that case it would be stupid for Millard to compound disaster by getting arrested for car theft.

He said, "Very well. Where is this inn?"

Chapter 29

What a strange dream he was having. In it he lay on the ground, staring up at a sky pink with sunrise. Or was it sunset? No, it must be sunrise, because he could hear birds singing. He could also hear a plane somewhere in the distance.

Joan sat beside him, gently pouring cold water onto his shoulder from a familiar-looking bottle. The cold water felt good—so good that he decided it was not a dream after all. She set down the bottle and smiled at him, although her eyes told him that she was very worried about something. He heard the sound of rustling paper. Then she held something to his lips. It looked and smelled like a chocolate.

He did not want it. He turned his head aside, closed his eyes, and went back to sleep.

Muffy, seated on a lap robe a few feet away, listened to that plane somewhere to the north. She still felt stunned by what Joan had told her a few minutes before. It had been on the car radio, a kidnap plot by some men in Moscow. Underneath her shock, though, she felt something like exhilaration. Imagine those men in Moscow—under arrest now, and it certainly served them right—imagine them considering her, Martha Matilda, important enough to kidnap.

And imagine them thinking they could ever persuade

her to say anything bad about Buzz or the men he had chosen for his Cabinet!

Of course, she thought uneasily, there was this brain-washing you heard about. And at times in the past she had wondered if Buzz was listening to the wrong men. Again she thought of those chanting young people.

Could it be that those Russians *could* have maneuvered her into making their nasty propaganda broadcast?

Oh, dear. Why was everything so complicated? When she was a little girl in Cleveland, she had thought good was good and bad was bad. But the older she grew, the more it seemed to her that good and bad were all mixed up together.

As for yesterday, she could understand now about the men with the rifle and the machine gun, and about the plane. But she still did not understand about Dan Manchester. Why had he suddenly gotten up from the road, when she'd been afraid he was already dead, and picked up that rifle and shot at Paul Lescaut? Had he suddenly gone crazy?

It had been a terrible experience for Joan to go through. But Muffy was glad that the gun had been there for the girl to pick up.

She looked over at Joan. The girl had finished bandaging the shoulder wound. Now she was looking down in Paul Lescaut's sleeping face. Why, Muffy thought, she's in love with him!

Muffy herself believed that like should marry like. The best marriages were when you actually had grown up together, the way she and Buzz had. At the very least, husbands and wives should be of the same nationality, and religion, and background. That was why she had thought it would be nice if Joan fell in love with someone like Dan Manchester—or, she amended hastily, someone like what Dan had seemed to be until yesterday.

Well, Paul Lescaut was a fine man, a really remarkable man. In spite of the nasty bump on the head he'd got when he slipped in that garage, and in spite of that double dose of pills Dan Manchester had given him—on purpose, probably!—yesterday he'd fought like— Well, he'd fought like a tiger.

One thing was certain. She herself had better not sit here on the ground much longer. It was sure to bring on her rheumatism. She dreaded the sight of those two men lying in the road, but just the same, after a while she was going to take some of the chocolates and go down to the car. She would lie down on the back seat, so that she couldn't see the road. If there were any more Russian hoodlums in these mountains, they wouldn't come near the Mercedes. Every radio in the country now must be blaring the news that their nasty scheme had collapsed, and that there were search planes in the air and patrol cars combing the roads.

Joan soaked the bandage with cold water several times that day. With growing hope she noticed that the area around the wound was less red. Late in the afternoon Paul opened his eyes. He had done so several times since early morning, but each time she had not been sure that he even recognized her. Now, with a surge of thankfulness, she saw that his gaze was clear, rational. He even smiled at her. She asked, "Are you feeling better?"

"Much better."

She held something to his lips. "It's chocolate filled with brandy. Better eat it if you can."

He swallowed the candy, enjoying the taste of the chocolate and the spurt of fiery liquid against the back of his throat. Then he closed his eyes and went back to sleep.

When he again awoke, twilight filled the clearing. A moon, a little larger than it had been the night before, floated in the patch of sky visible above the pines. Again he heard a plane, this time some distance to the south. Placing the palm of his left hand on the ground, he hoisted himself to a sitting position.

Joan got up from the lap robe pallet where she sat and hurried to him. "Should you be sitting up?"

"Yes." He still felt weak, and his shoulder hurt. But his mind was clear, and his headache had gone entirely. He was going to be all right—physically, at least.

He looked around the clearing. "Where is she?"

"Muffy?" Joan sat down beside him. "She went back to the car. The last time I went down there she was reading *Lorna Doone*. It's all right," she added quickly. "No one is going to try anything now, not with planes and patrol cars searching this whole area for us."

She told him then of the radio broadcasts she had heard that day. The President's statement announcing the disappearance of the former President's widow, and emphasizing that only a very small faction in Russia was responsible. The Chairman of the Politburo's statement telling of the arrest of four members of that body, and of the continuing search, both in Budapest and the Austrian Alps, for the ex-President's widow and her companions.

"I can't see why they haven't found us. Time and again I've thought a plane was going to fly right over the valley, but always it veered off."

"There are a lot of Alps, and a lot of valleys. In a few minutes I will make sure that they do find us."

"How?"

"I will heap dead branches and anything else I can find

178

under that plane, and then set fire to it."

She nodded. "I'll help you."

"All right." After a few moments he said, "I did not know it until yesterday, but Manchester must have been in on it from the very first."

She felt suddenly frightened, not by what he had said, but by a sense that in a moment he would say something she did not want to hear. It was several seconds before she answered, "I realize he must have been. That was why he asked to be assigned to Muffy."

"I was in on it, too. At least I had to pretend to go along with it." His voice was toneless. "I have been in Russian pay for the last ten years. They gave me twenty thousand francs a year for carrying messages. Although I did not realize it, they were also paying me to stand by until they had some real use for me."

He forced himself to turn his head and meet her look —that look of stunned revulsion he had known he would see. Then she averted her face. He waited for perhaps a minute, but she neither spoke nor moved.

Reaching over to the flight bag, he took out the flashlight, and then struggled to his feet. He said with no expression whatsoever, "I will go down and set that fire now."

She heard him slide awkwardly down the slope to the path. Still she did not move.

From the very first, she had sensed that because of something in his life he had been set apart from other men. On that little island in the lagoon, she had thought she had learned what that something was. Yesterday, though, she had begun to feel there was more than what he had told her. When he turned off the highway onto that rough "shortcut," and then onto that even rougher track beside the stream, he had seemed to her that he was

179

a man acting under some sort of terrible duress.

Last night and today she had shied away from thinking about it. But even if she had thought about it, she would never have suspected the ugly fact of that twenty thousand francs a year. Twenty thousand for living in the shadows, at the bidding of ruthless men willing to kidnap and murder to gain their goals.

But in the end, he had not done their bidding. Already weakened, he had defied and shot down two armed men, and then nearly lost his life to a third man.

She thought, too, of the young Paul Lescaut she had never known, searching for—and finding—his beloved wife and little girl there among the thatched-roof huts. Something within him also must have died then, perhaps the ability to have faith in any sort of society. Was it so strange that he had turned into a nihilist—cold, withdrawn, utterly cynical about the powerful men of the world and the governments they led?

She drew up her knees, rested her cheek on them, and wrapped her arms around her legs. She should have gone with him. She thought of him making his way down into the valley, one arm dangling uselessly at his side, then laboriously gathering material for his fire, and then climbing up to the road again. Well, it was too late now for her to follow him. He had taken the flashlight, and with no light except that of the moon she would never be able to find her way down the steep, rocky slope to the valley.

An explosive roar. She lifted her head and looked to her right. Even from here she could see, through the trees, the wavering glow cast upward by the flames on the runway. So he had done it.

Only a few minutes later, she heard an approaching plane. From its sound she knew that it had begun to circle over the valley, its revved engine signaling that the

180

pilot had seen the burning plane. Then it flew off.

Time stretched out. What seemed to her at least another fifteen minutes passed. Fear became a tight band around her chest. Perhaps something had gone wrong. Perhaps he had been too close when the plane's fuel tank exploded.

Then she heard him climbing the bank. She got to her feet. He said, "You heard the plane circling. There will be patrol cars here soon."

"Paul—"

"Before I went down to the landing strip, I stopped by the car and told your cousin what I was going to do, so that she would not be frightened."

"Paul, listen to me! I understand why you did it. It wasn't just for the money. It was because of what happened to your wife and child. In a way, you died too, so that after that nothing made any real difference to—"

"Perhaps. But I did it, and at this late date it does not matter why."

"It matters to me!" Her voice broke. "Oh, Paul! I love you so much!"

When he spoke, his voice was harsh. "Then you had better start not loving me, because I am going to prison, and probably for quite a few years."

"You're not; you're not. Why, yesterday—"

"Yesterday will not count, at least not enough. I am a Frenchman, and for the last ten years I have been breaking French law, which is a very dangerous thing to do."

"Paul! The French won't need to know, at least not until you're safe in America. After what you've done for Muffy, the Americans would never allow the French to get their hands on—"

"The French government already knows about me. Perhaps, if I had been able to get us all out of Austria yesterday— But I did not, and by now there must be French security police here in Austria ready to arrest me."

After a moment she whispered, "The French police know about you? How is it that they—"

"In Florence there's a woman named Carlotta. I rent a room in her flat. The night before we left Florence I wrote out a full account of the kidnap plan, including how I became involved in it."

She whispered, "Oh, Paul!"

"I gave the envelope to Carlotta. I told her to keep it until she heard from me. Before we left Venice yesterday morning, I telephoned her and told her that if she did not hear from me again within twelve hours, she was to take the envelope to the police there in Florence. She must have done so last night. You can bet that the Florence police lost no time in getting in touch with the Sûreté in Paris."

"But why?" She was crying now. "Why did you do it, darling?"

"Because I did not know whether or not I could save you, save all of us. All of us," he said ironically, "including Manchester. And if we were to be killed, I did not want those bastards who had been giving me orders to get away with it."

Still crying, she moved close to him. His good arm went around her, and they kissed with a kind of hungry despair.

From the direction of the highway came the sound of sirens. He held her tightly for a moment more and then said, "They are coming. We might as well walk down to meet them."

Chapter 30

Standing at the window, Joan stared listlessly down at the willow tree in the back yard of the apartment house opposite. It was August now, and the willow's branches seemed to trail even more limply in the merciless New York heat.

More than three months had passed since the night—or rather, early morning—when she had parted from Paul near the reception desk of that Salzburg hospital. Someone—to this day she could not remember whether it had been a hospital staff member or one of the Austrian police—had told her to come back at ten. Escorted by two Austrian security men, she and Muffy had gone to a hotel for the night. At nine-thirty the next morning, heedless of the beauty of the medieval town in its cup of snow-capped mountains, she had taken a taxi to the hospital, only to be told that Paul was not there. At daylight, after the bullet had been removed from his shoulder, two French officials with extradition papers had taken him to the airport.

Back at the hotel, Muffy had tried to comfort her. "We'll go to Paris. The French won't hold him. He'll come to America with us. You'll see. Why, it's ridiculous that they should try to keep him locked up, after all he did."

Leaving Austria was not all that simple. There were

American State Department officials and CIA men on the scene by that time, and they, like the Austrian police, had endless questions to ask about that afternoon on the dirt road above the long-unused landing strip, and about Dan Manchester and Paul Lescaut. But as Muffy said, at least all those officials kept the newspaper people off their necks.

When they did get to Paris three days later, accompanied by two State Department men impatient to get them to safety in America, they found they still could not see Paul. In a big, sunny office overlooking the Seine, a high-ranking and very polite French Intelligence official told them that Paul was under police guard at a hospital. No, he was not at liberty to say which hospital. Yes, naturally the court would take into consideration Monsieur Lescaut's admirable behavior during that truly deplorable affair in Austria. And yes, naturally they were grateful for Monsieur Lescaut's information about other Russian agents who had been operating in France. Already they had taken into custody the man Lescaut knew as Millard, along with two companions. They hoped to arrest others soon.

Naturally, too, France was always pleased when it could oblige its great friend and ally, the United States of America. But this was a matter of French internal security, and therefore French justice must take its course.

"Don't you worry," Muffy said, as she and Joan emerged from the marble building into the weak Paris sunshine. "I'll go to Washington as soon as we get home. The President will make it hot for stubborn people like that man back there, or else I'll give him a piece of my mind. Why, it was Buzz who gave the President his start. Buzz was in the Senate then, and the President was a wet-behind-the-ears law school graduate. Buzz chose him for his staff."

Muffy had been down to Washington twice in the last few months. Both times she had reported to Joan that she felt the President and the State Department were doing all they could do. But so far American pressure upon the proudly intransigent French had not brought Paul's release. Three times he had written to her. The letters, which she could see had been heavily censored, had said that he was well, that he did not know when he would be brought to trial, and that he hoped she was considering her own future.

The phone rang. Probably it was Eileen Haskel again. Even though it was a Saturday, her boss already had called her twice about the January issue. Joan suspected that the calls were prompted, not by an acute anxiety about the January issue, but by Eileen's conviction that it was better for a woman to work herself into a nervous breakdown than to brood herself into one.

Joan lifted the phone. "Hello."

"Miss Joan Creighton? We have a Paris call for you."

She waited, heart pounding. Then he said, "Joan? Joan?"

For a moment she couldn't speak. "Paul? Is it—"

"Yes, my darling, it is. And I am free. I think now that they never intended to bring me to trial."

Joy held her silent for several seconds. Then she cried, "But why, then? Why did they hold you so long?"

"We French are a proud-necked race." How young he sounded, and how close, almost as if he were across the street. "They did not want to give in too soon to the mighty Uncle Sam. But I am free now, and your State Department has issued me a visa, and I am coming to America."

"When?"

"Next Wednesday, on the noon plane. Also—and I suspect I have your State Department to thank for this too—I have job offers."

"What sort of jobs?"

"Teaching French."

She said dazedly, "Teaching!"

"Yes. I have always thought I would enjoy teaching."

She laughed. "I didn't know that about you. There's so much I don't know about you. Where are you going to teach?"

"One offer is from a college in Connecticut, and the other from a women's college in— It is a very peculiar name, probably of American Indian origin. Pokipli, or something like that."

"Poughkeepsie. That's Vassar! Turn that offer down!" She felt giddy with happiness. "I will not have you teaching in a girls' school."

"Oh, Joan." His voice had roughened. "The things I have to say to you."

"You can start saying them at the airport on Wednesday."

"You will be there to meet me?"

"What do you think?" she said. "What do you think?"